DC SUPER HERO GIRLS™

HITS AND MYTHS

an original graphic novel

WRITTEN BY
Shea Fontana

ART BY
Yancey Labat

COLORS BY
Monica Kubina

LETTERING BY
Janice Chiang

D0513278

MARIE JAVINS Editor
BRITTANY HOLZHERR Assistant Editor
STEVE COOK Design Director - Books
AMIE BROCKWAY-METCALF Publication Design

BOB HARRAS Senior VP - Editor-in-Chief, DC Comics

DIANE NELSON President
DAN DIDIO Publisher
JIM LEE Publisher
GEOFF JOHNS President & Chief Creative Officer
AMIT DESAI Executive VP - Business & Marketing Strategy, Direct to Consumer & Global Franchise Management
SAM ADES Senior VP - Direct to Consumer
BOBBIE CHASE VP - Talent Development
MARK CHIARELLO Senior VP - Art, Design & Collected Editions
JOHN CUNNINGHAM Senior VP - Sales & Trade Marketing
ANNE DEPIES Senior VP - Business Strategy, Finance & Administration
DON FALLETTI VP - Manufacturing Operations
LAWRENCE GANEM VP - Editorial Administration & Talent Relations
ALISON GILL Senior VP - Manufacturing & Operations
HANK KANALZ Senior VP - Editorial Strategy & Administration
JAY KOGAN VP - Legal Affairs
THOMAS LOFTUS VP - Business Affairs
JACK MAHAN VP - Business Affairs
NICK J. NAPOLITANO VP - Manufacturing Administration
EDDIE SCANNELL VP - Consumer Marketing
COURTNEY SIMMONS Senior VP - Publicity & Communications
JIM (SKI) SOKOLOWSKI VP - Comic Book Specialty Sales & Trade Marketing
NANCY SPEARS VP - Mass, Book, Digital Sales & Trade Marketing

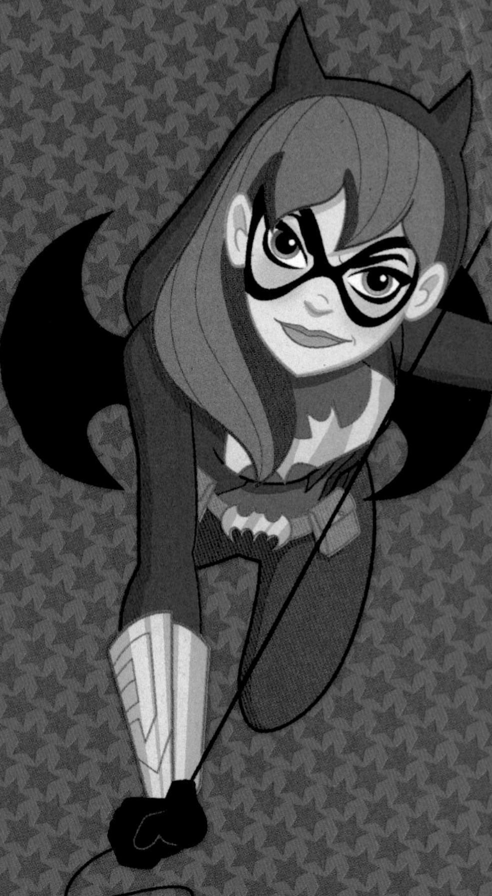

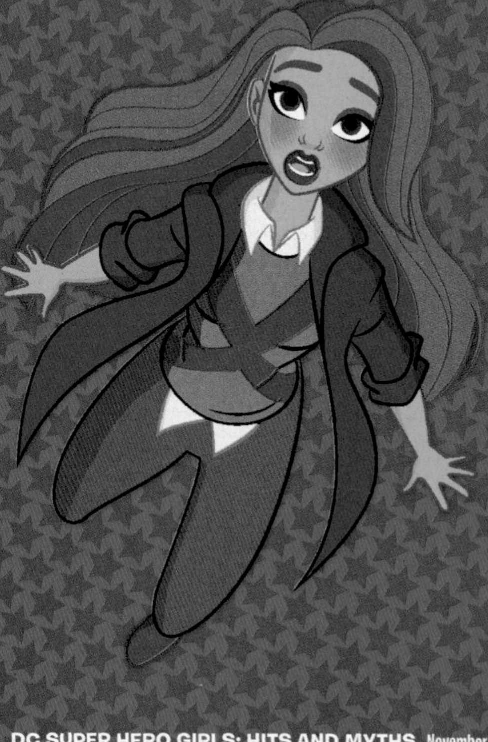

DC SUPER HERO GIRLS: HITS AND MYTHS. November, 2016. Published by DC Comics, 2900 W. Alameda Avenue, Burbank, CA 91505. GST # is R125921072. This book is manufactured at a facility holding chain-of-custody certification. This paper is made with sustainably managed North American fiber. For Advertising and Custom Publishing contact dccomicsadvertising@dccomics.com. For details on DC Comics Ratings, visit dccomics.com/go/ratings. Printed by Transcontinental Interglobe, Beauceville, QC, Canada. 9/30/16. ISBN: 978-1-4012-6761-2

PEFC Certified
Printed on paper from sustainably managed forests and controlled sources
PEFC
PEFC/01-31-106
www.pefc.org

TABLE OF CONTENTS

Roll Call 4

The Journey 7

The Cyclops 26

The Witch 45

The Sirens 64

The Underworld 83

The Return Home 104

ROLL

SUPER HERO HIGH SCHOOL

S H H S

WONDER WOMAN

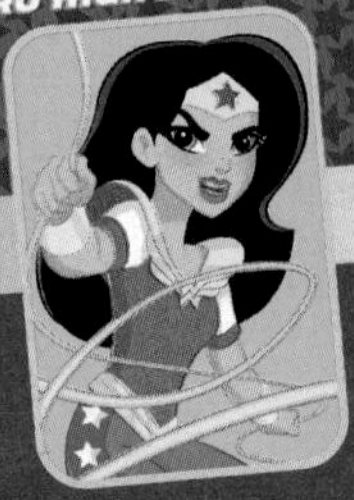

SUPERPOWERS

Super-strength, flight, near-invincibility, super-athleticism

SUPER HERO HIGH SCHOOL

S H H S

SUPERGIRL

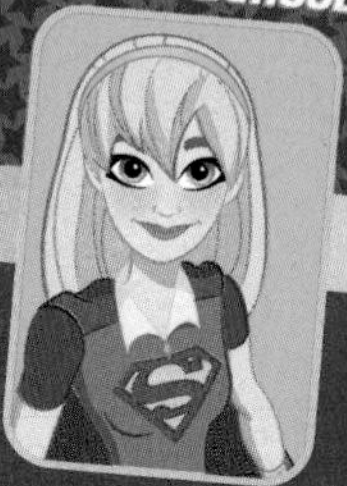

SUPERPOWERS

Super-strength, flight, invincibility, super-hearing, heat vision, x-ray vision

SUPER HERO HIGH SCHOOL

S H H S

BATGIRL

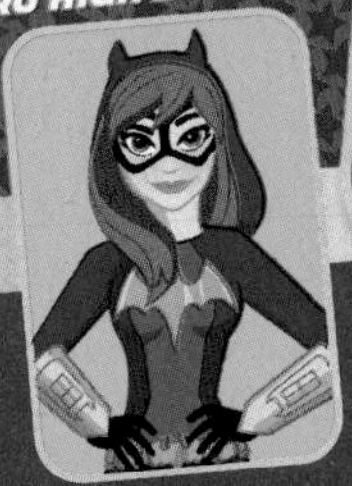

SUPERPOWERS

Computer genius, expert martial artist, photographic memory, legendary detective skills

SUPER HERO HIGH SCHOOL

S H H S

BUMBLEBEE

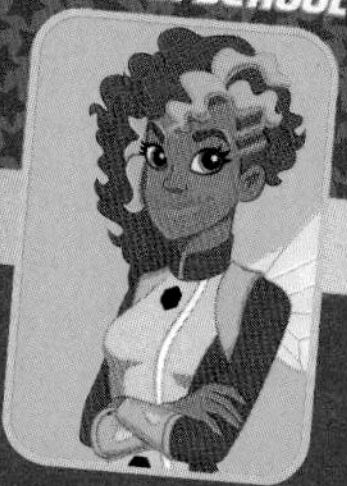

SUPERPOWERS

Enhanced strength, flight, ability to shrink, projects stinger blasts

SUPER HERO HIGH SCHOOL

S H H S

POISON IVY

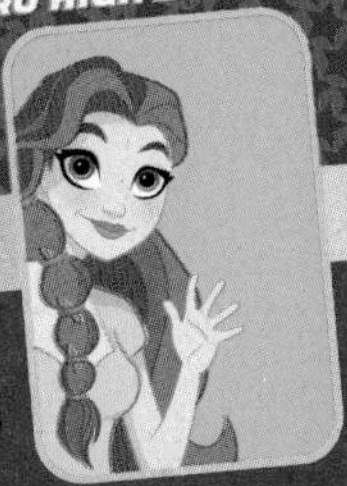

SUPERPOWERS

Genius-level intellect, summons and controls plants

SUPER HERO HIGH SCHOOL

S H H S

HARLEY QUINN

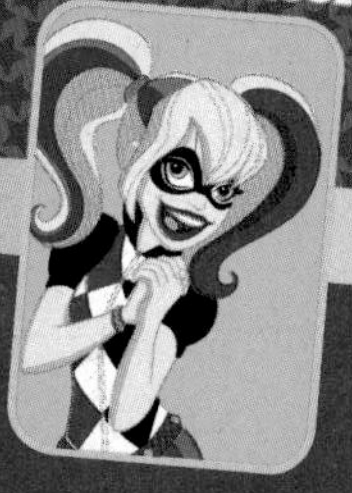

SUPERPOWERS

Expert gymnast, acrobat, quick-witted class clown

SUPER HERO HIGH SCHOOL

S H H S

KATANA

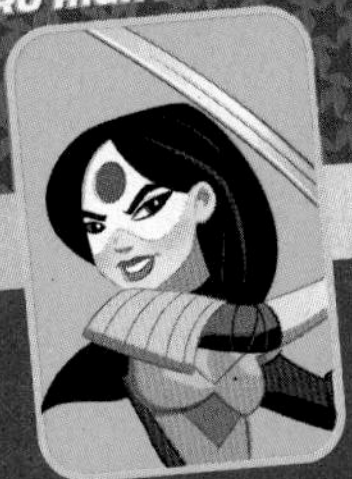

SUPERPOWERS

Superior sword-fighter, expert martial artist, advanced stealth skills

SUPER HERO HIGH SCHOOL

S H H S

BEAST BOY

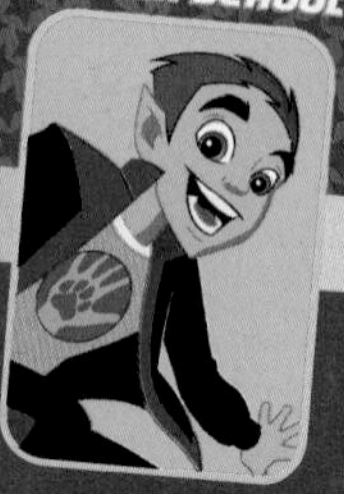

SUPERPOWERS

Shape-shifts into any animal form, world-class slacker

SUPER HERO HIGH SCHOOL

S H H S

CHEETAH

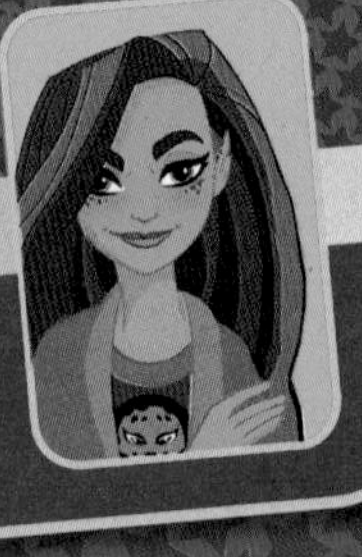

SUPERPOWERS

Agility, speed, sharp reflexes, even sharper claws

CALL

SUPER HERO HIGH SCHOOL

SHHS

SILVER BANSHEE

SUPERPOWERS

Supernatural destructive scream, accelerated healing, flight

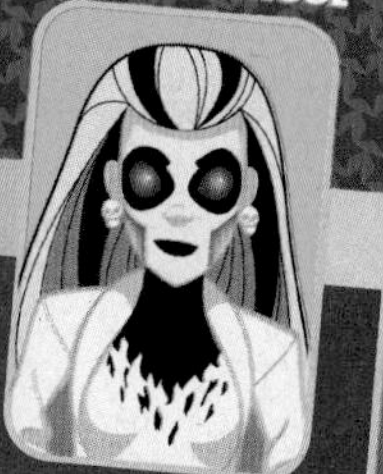

SUPER HERO HIGH SCHOOL

SHHS

FLASH

SUPERPOWERS

Super-speed, vibrates his molecules through walls, detective skills

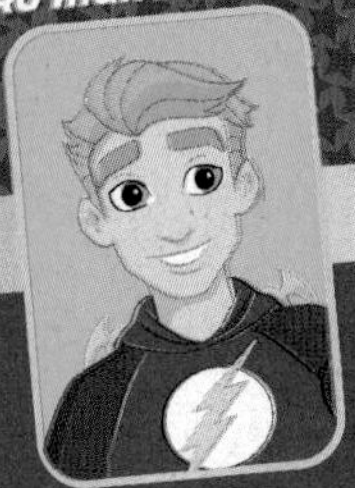

SUPER HERO HIGH SCHOOL

SHHS

RAVAGER

SUPERPOWERS

Advanced hand-to-hand combat, double-swords expert

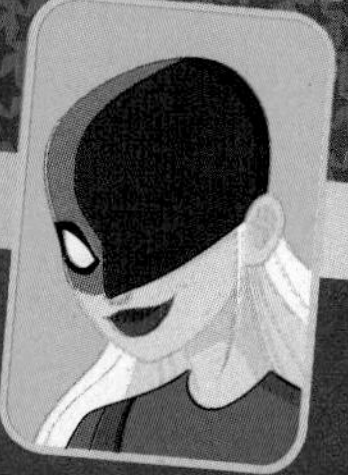

SUPER HERO HIGH SCHOOL

SHHS

HAWKGIRL

SUPERPOWERS

Flight, super detective skills, weapons expert

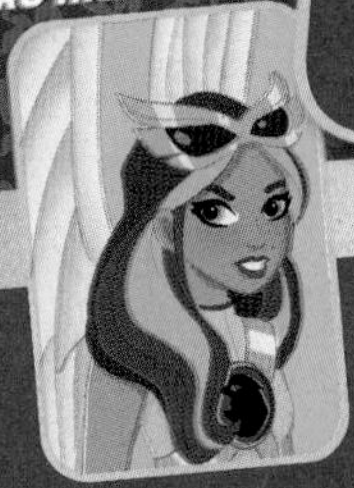

SUPER HERO HIGH SCHOOL

SHHS

MISS MARTIAN

SUPERPOWERS

Flight, shape-shifting, mind-reading, invisibility, super-strength

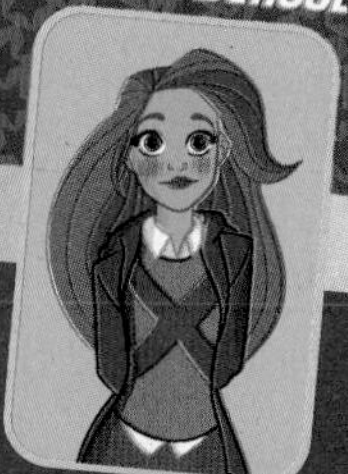

SUPER HERO HIGH SCHOOL

SHHS

AMANDA WALLER

Principal, mentor, stern but fair

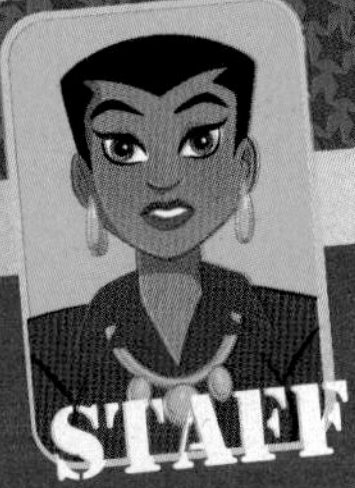
STAFF

SUPER HERO HIGH SCHOOL

SHHS

GORILLA GRODD

Vice Principal, mind-control powers, in charge of detention

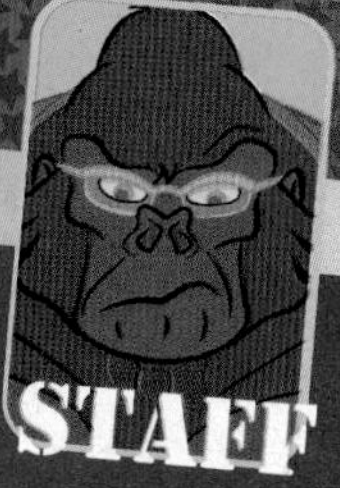
STAFF

SUPER HERO HIGH SCHOOL

SHHS

ETRIGAN

Professor of Poetry, not just *A* demon, *The* Demon!

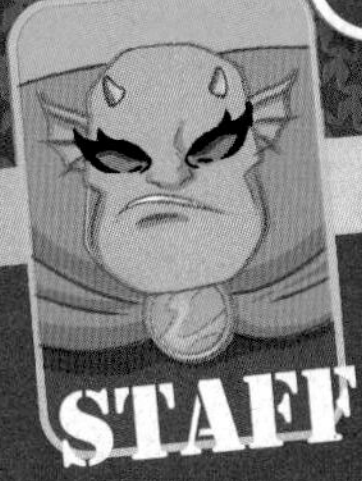
STAFF

SUPER HERO HIGH SCHOOL

SHHS

JUNE MOONE

Professor of Art, magical enchantress

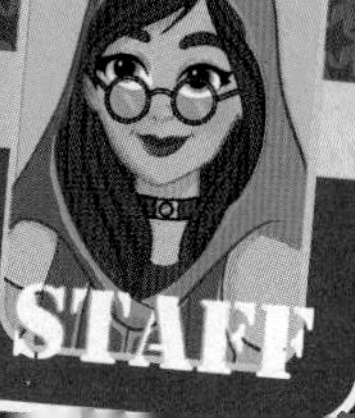
STAFF

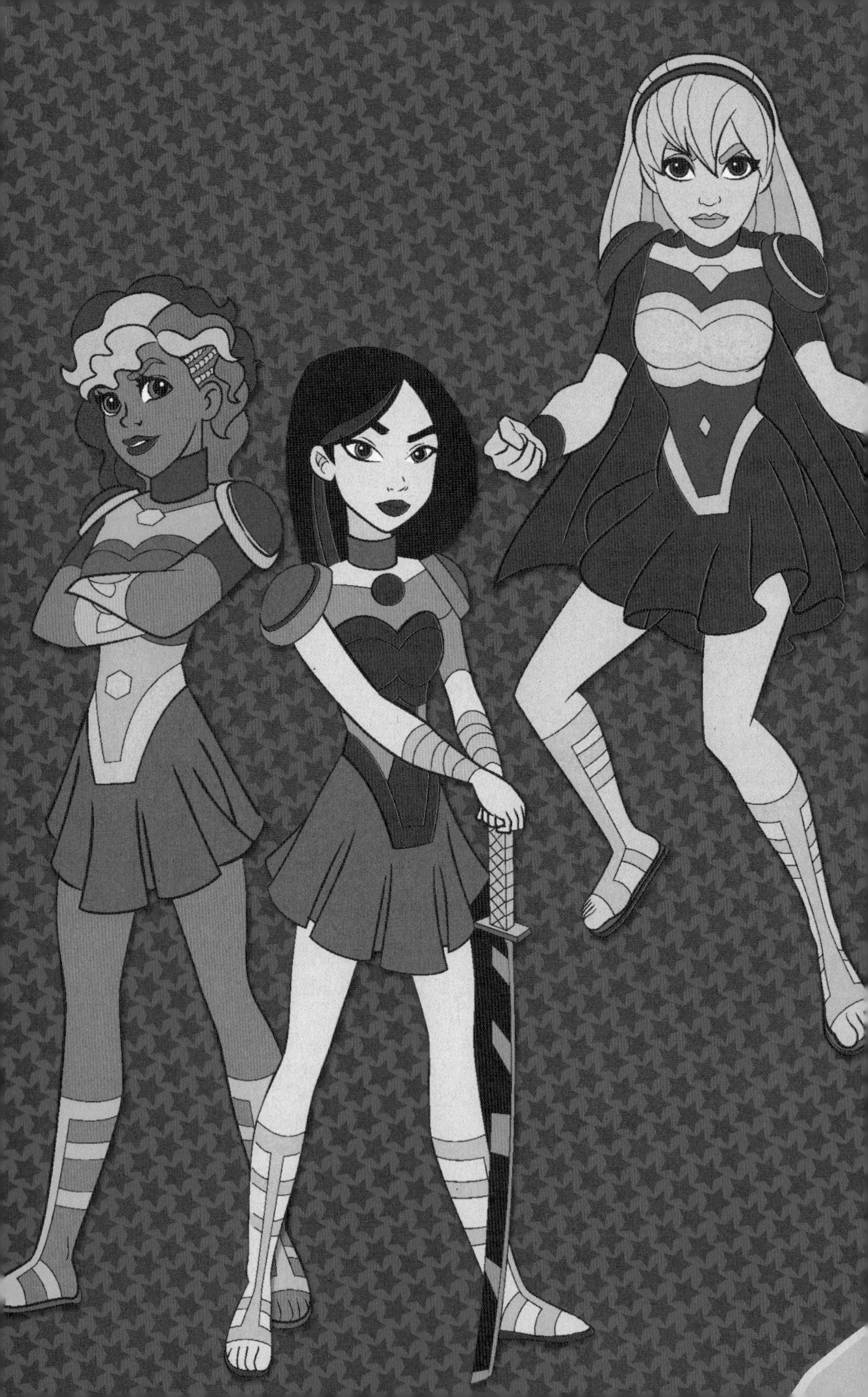

CHAPTER ONE
THE JOURNEY

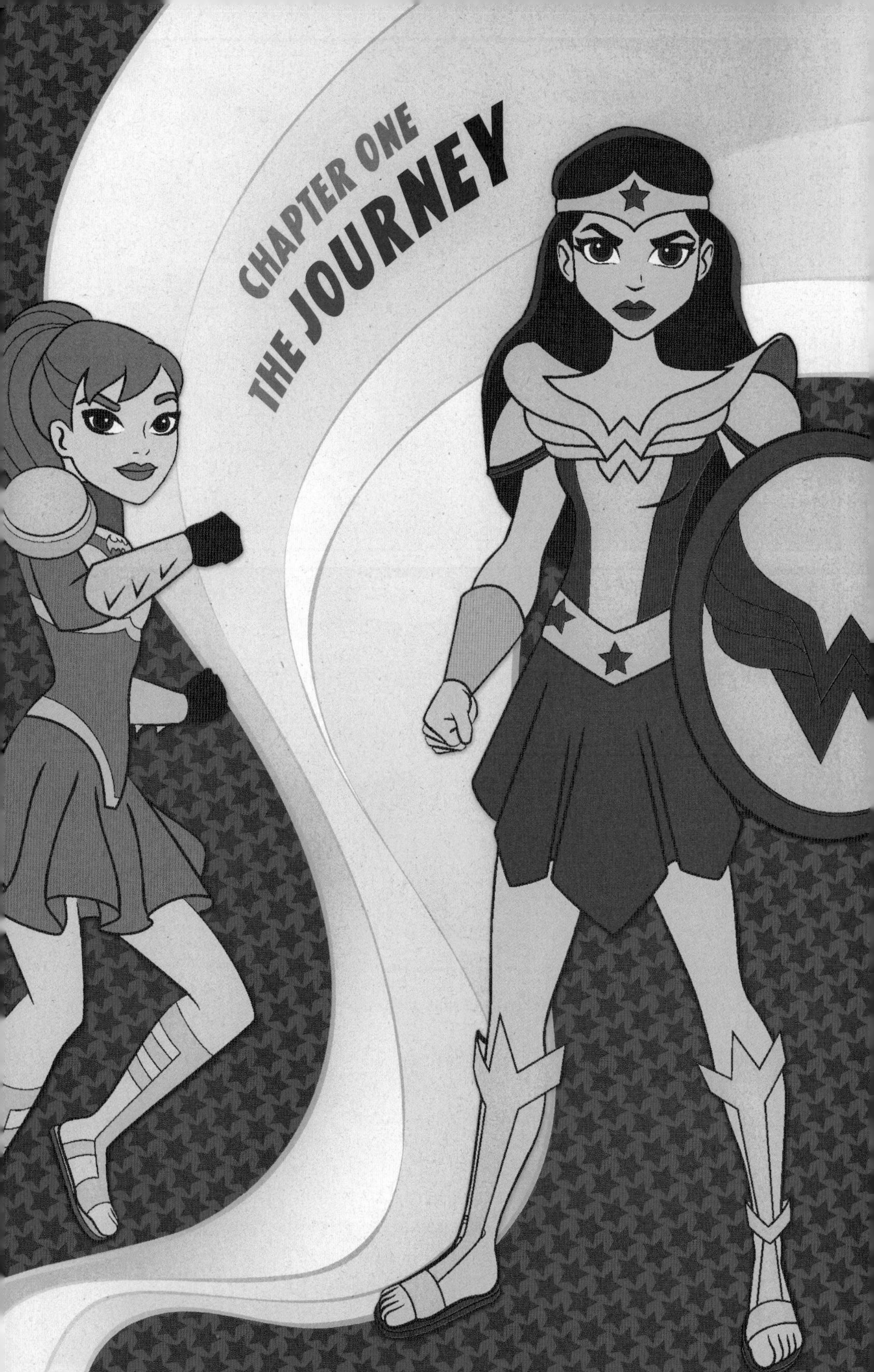

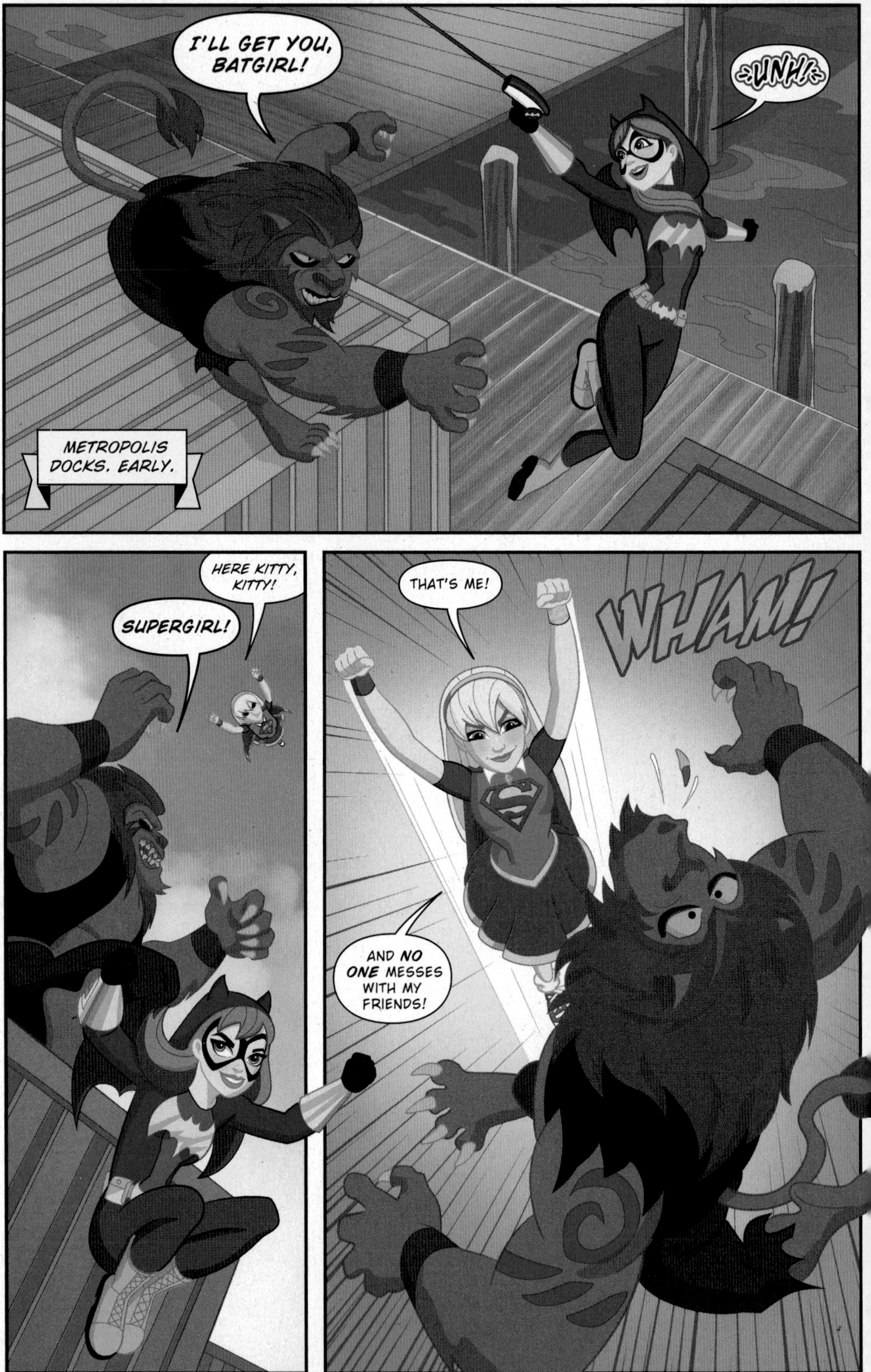
I'LL GET YOU, BATGIRL!
UNH!
METROPOLIS DOCKS. EARLY.
SUPERGIRL!
HERE KITTY, KITTY!
THAT'S ME!
WHAM!
AND NO ONE MESSES WITH MY FRIENDS!

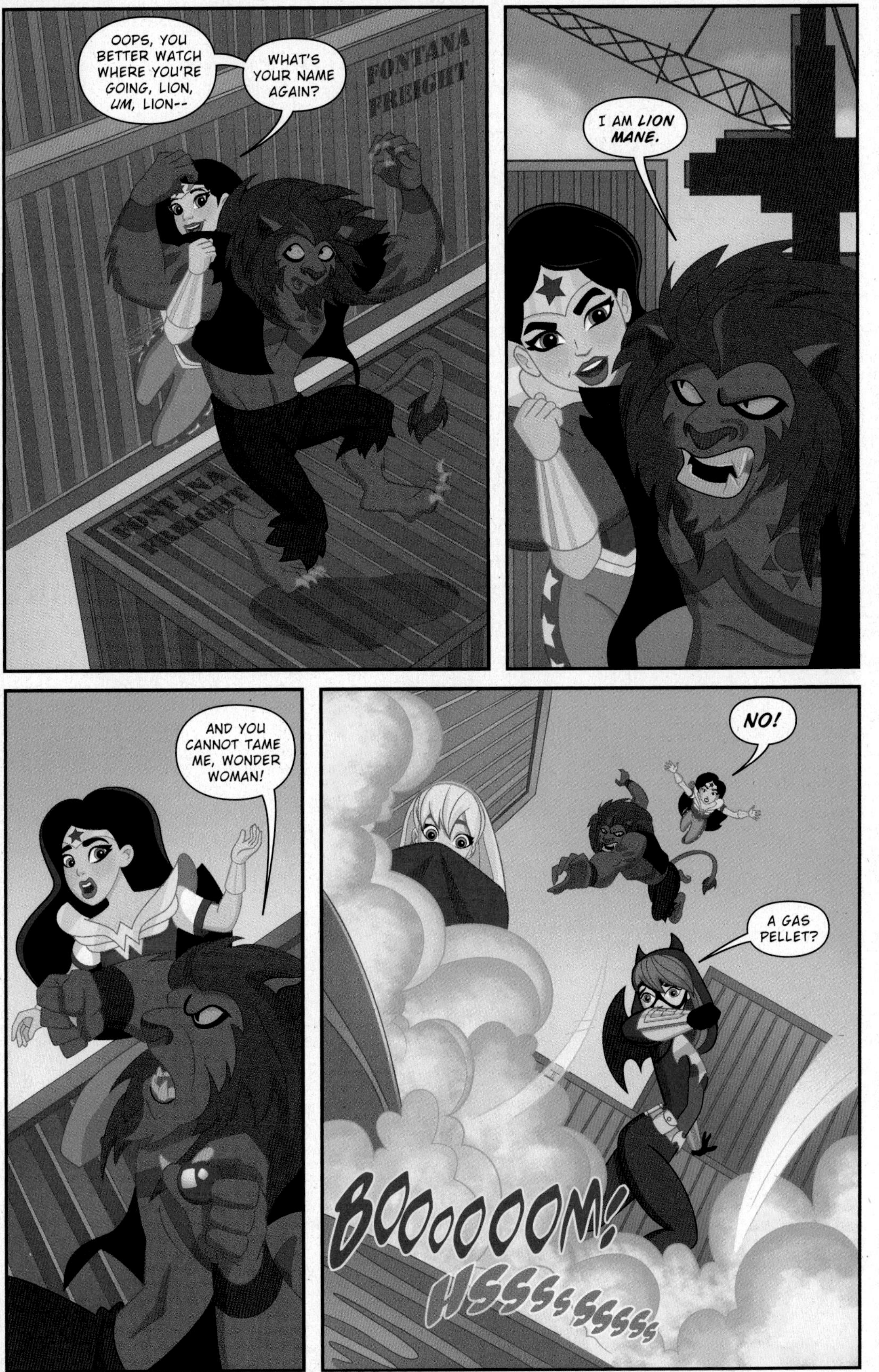
FONTANA FREIGHT
OOPS, YOU BETTER WATCH WHERE YOU'RE GOING, LION, UM, LION--
WHAT'S YOUR NAME AGAIN?
FONTANA FREIGHT
I AM LION MANE.
AND YOU CANNOT TAME ME, WONDER WOMAN!
NO!
A GAS PELLET?
BOOOOOOM!
HSSSSSSSSS

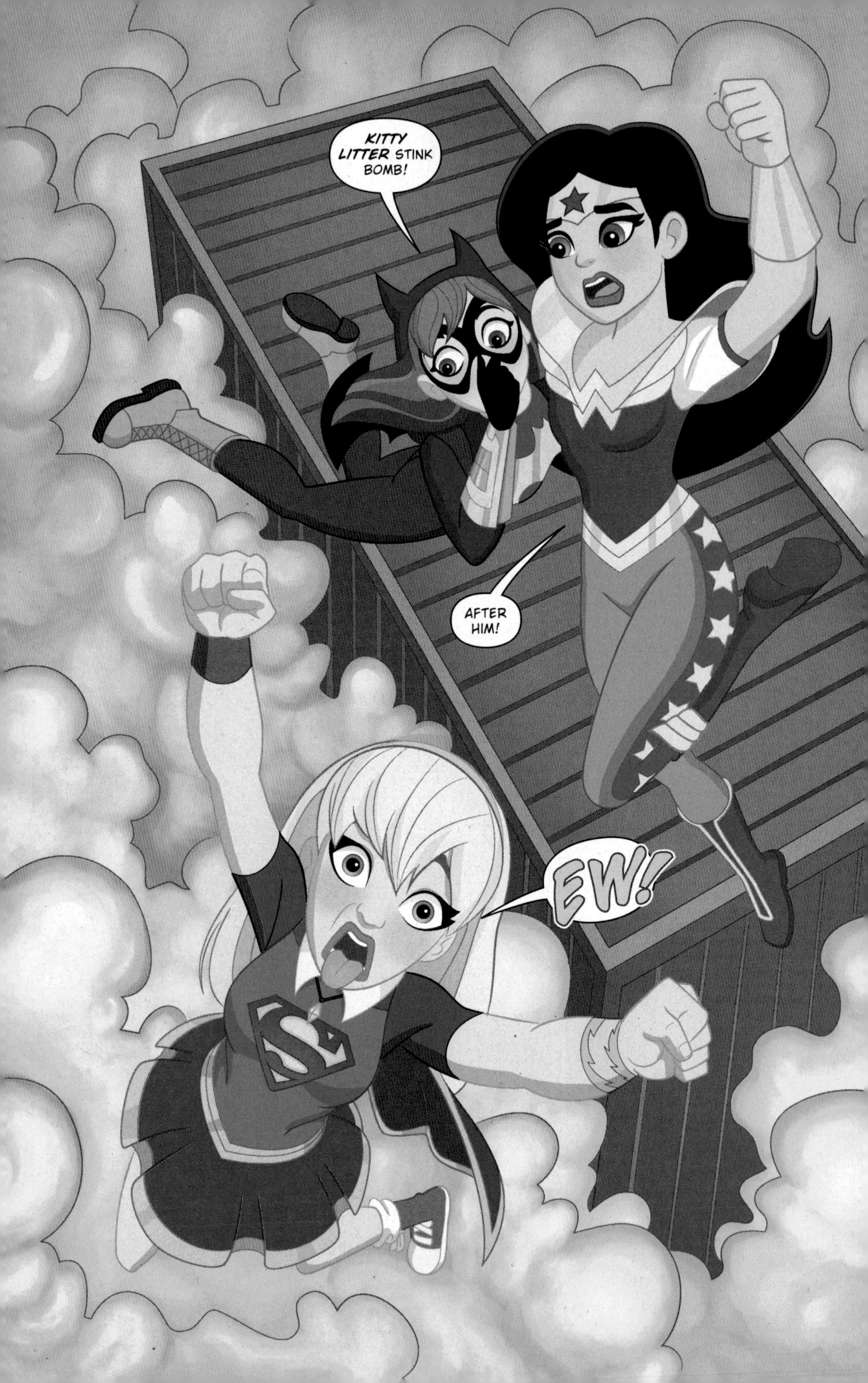
KITTY LITTER STINK BOMB!
AFTER HIM!
EW!

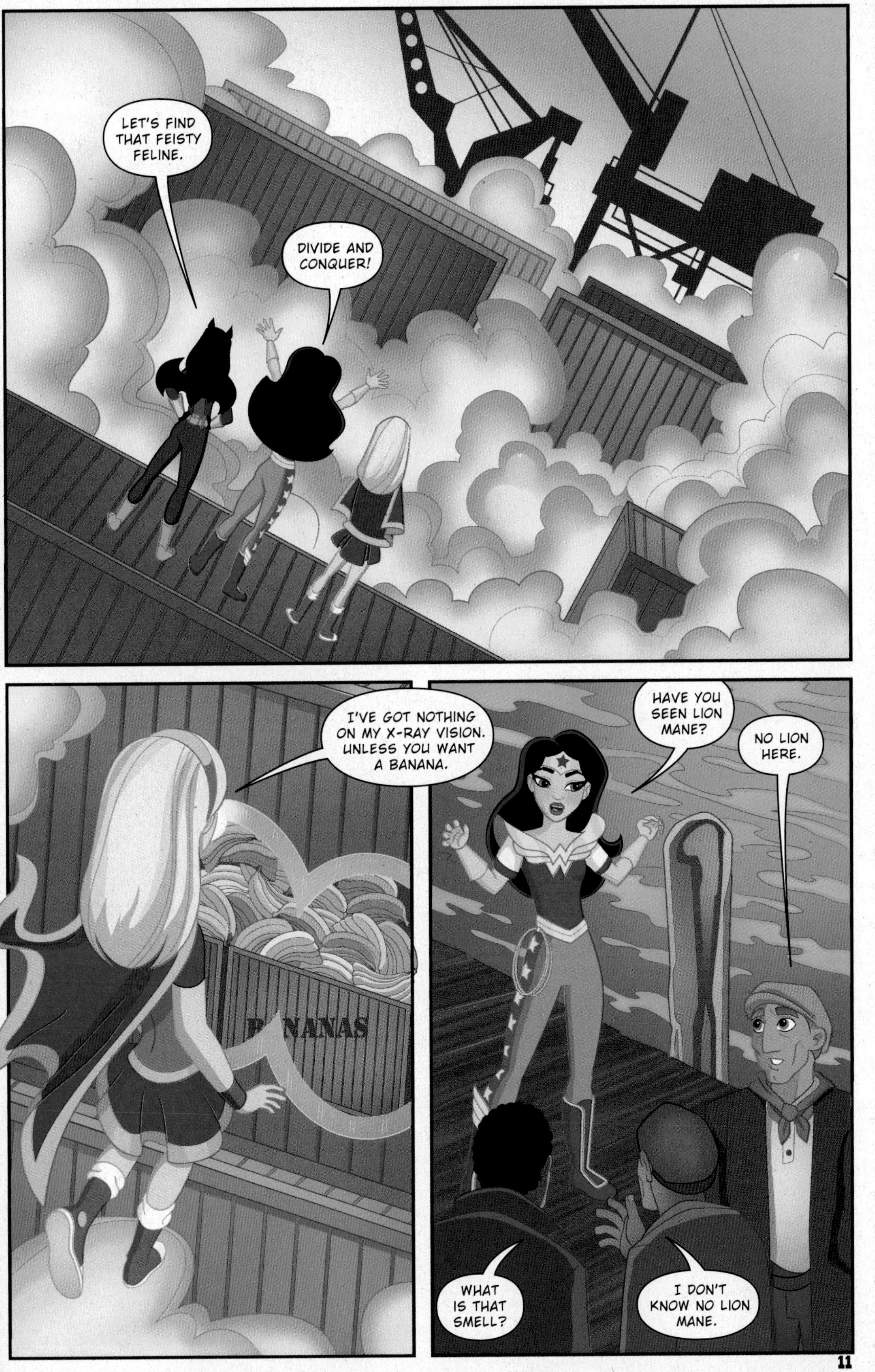

LET'S FIND THAT FEISTY FELINE.
DIVIDE AND CONQUER!
I'VE GOT NOTHING ON MY X-RAY VISION. UNLESS YOU WANT A BANANA.
BANANAS
HAVE YOU SEEN LION MANE?
NO LION HERE.
WHAT IS THAT SMELL?
I DON'T KNOW NO LION MANE.

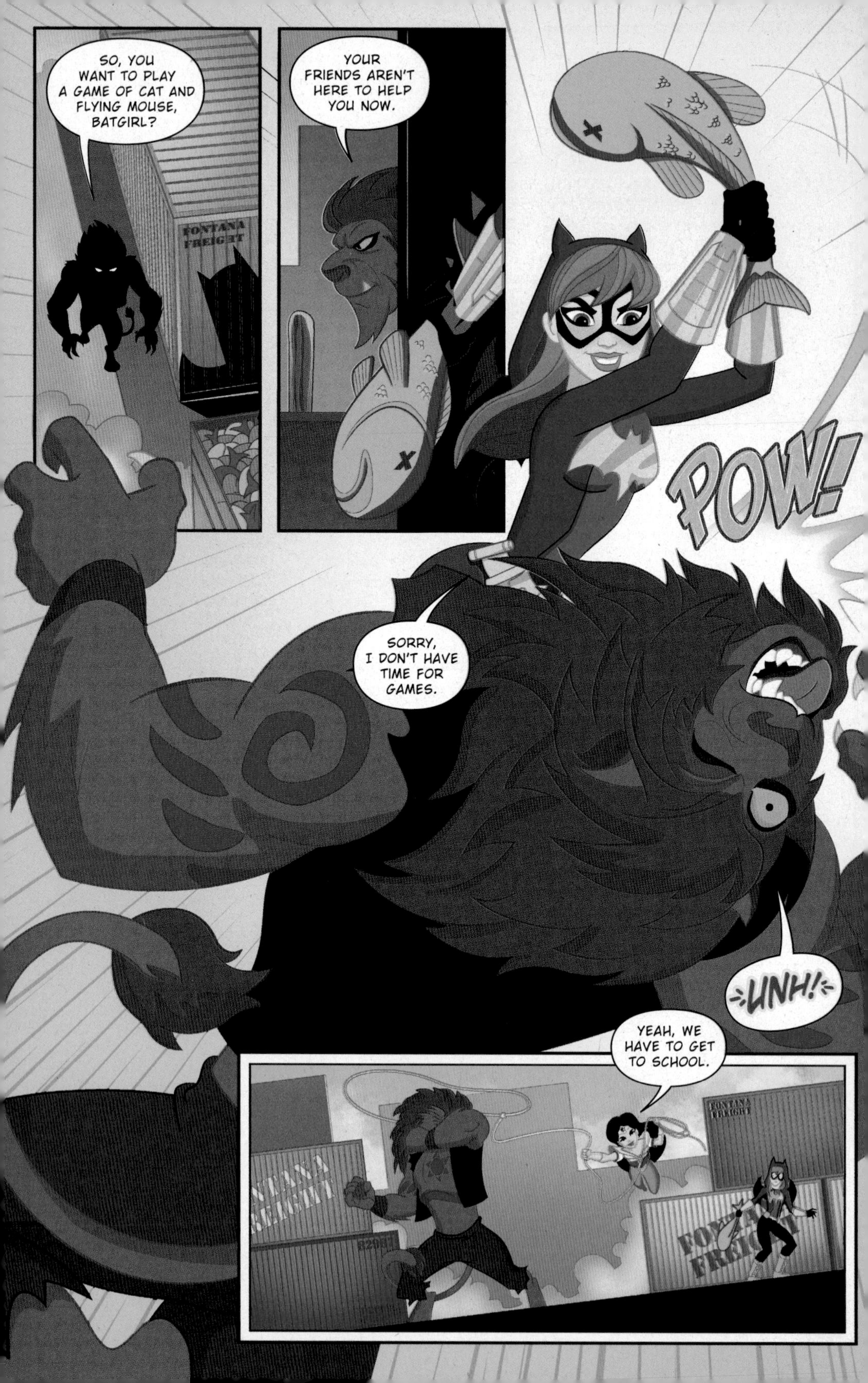
SO, YOU WANT TO PLAY A GAME OF CAT AND FLYING MOUSE, BATGIRL?
FONTANA FREIGHT
YOUR FRIENDS AREN'T HERE TO HELP YOU NOW.
POW!
SORRY, I DON'T HAVE TIME FOR GAMES.
UNH!
YEAH, WE HAVE TO GET TO SCHOOL.
FONTANA FREIGHT
FONTANA FREIGHT
FONTANA FREIGHT

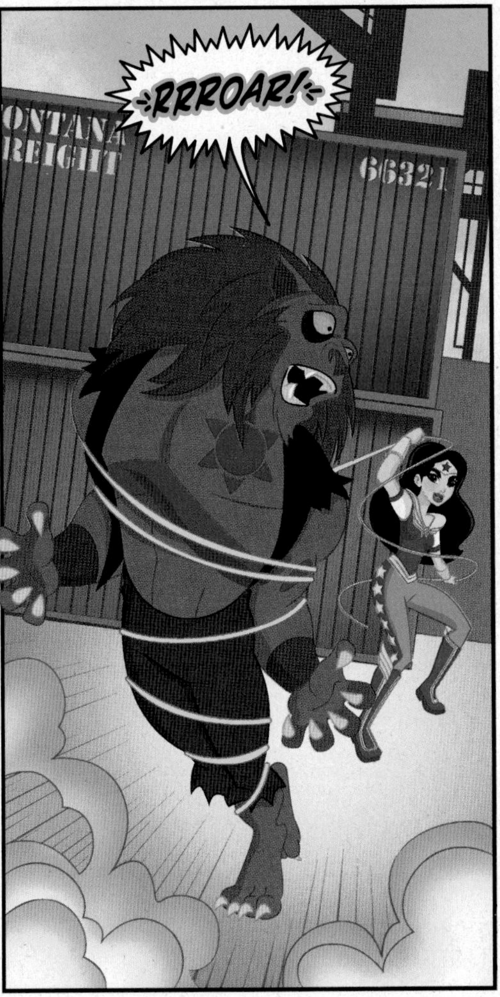
RRROAR!
ONTANA
REIGHT
66321

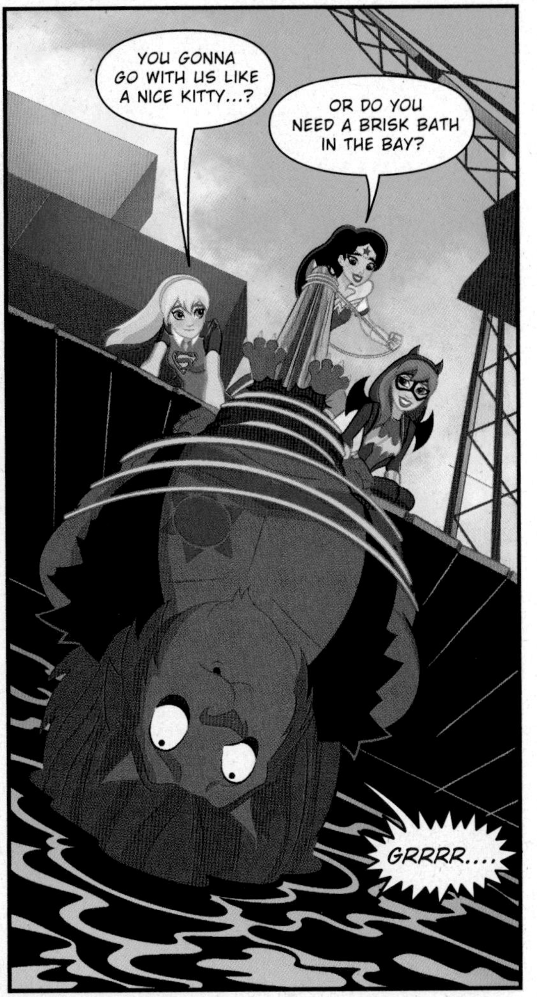
YOU GONNA GO WITH US LIKE A NICE KITTY...?
OR DO YOU NEED A BRISK BATH IN THE BAY?
GRRRR....

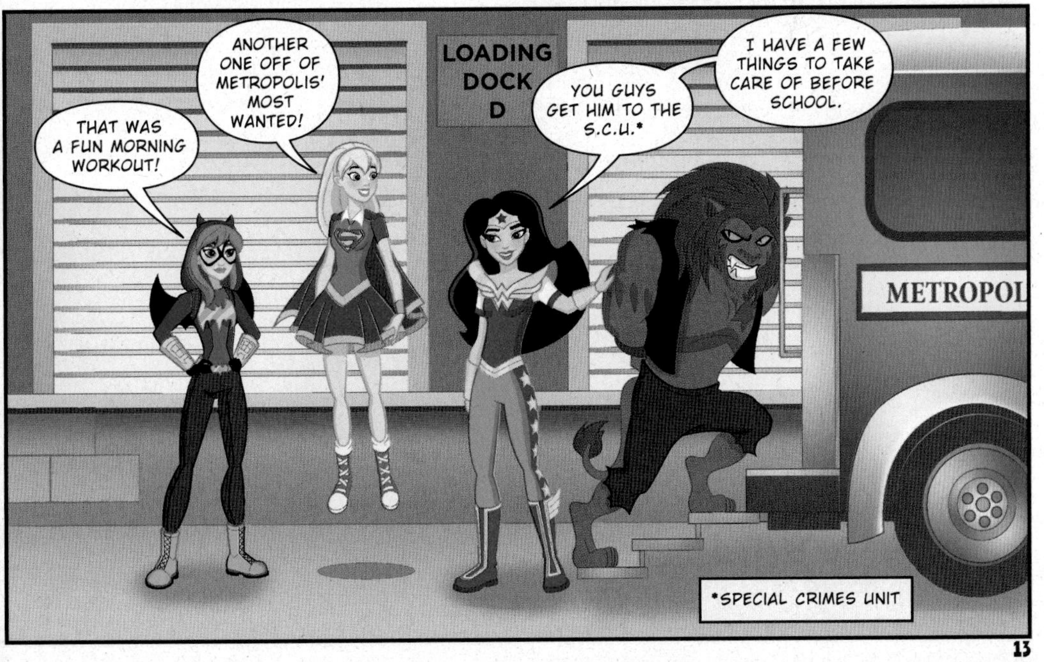
LOADING DOCK D
THAT WAS A FUN MORNING WORKOUT!
ANOTHER ONE OFF OF METROPOLIS' MOST WANTED!
YOU GUYS GET HIM TO THE S.C.U.*
I HAVE A FEW THINGS TO TAKE CARE OF BEFORE SCHOOL.
METROPOL
*SPECIAL CRIMES UNIT

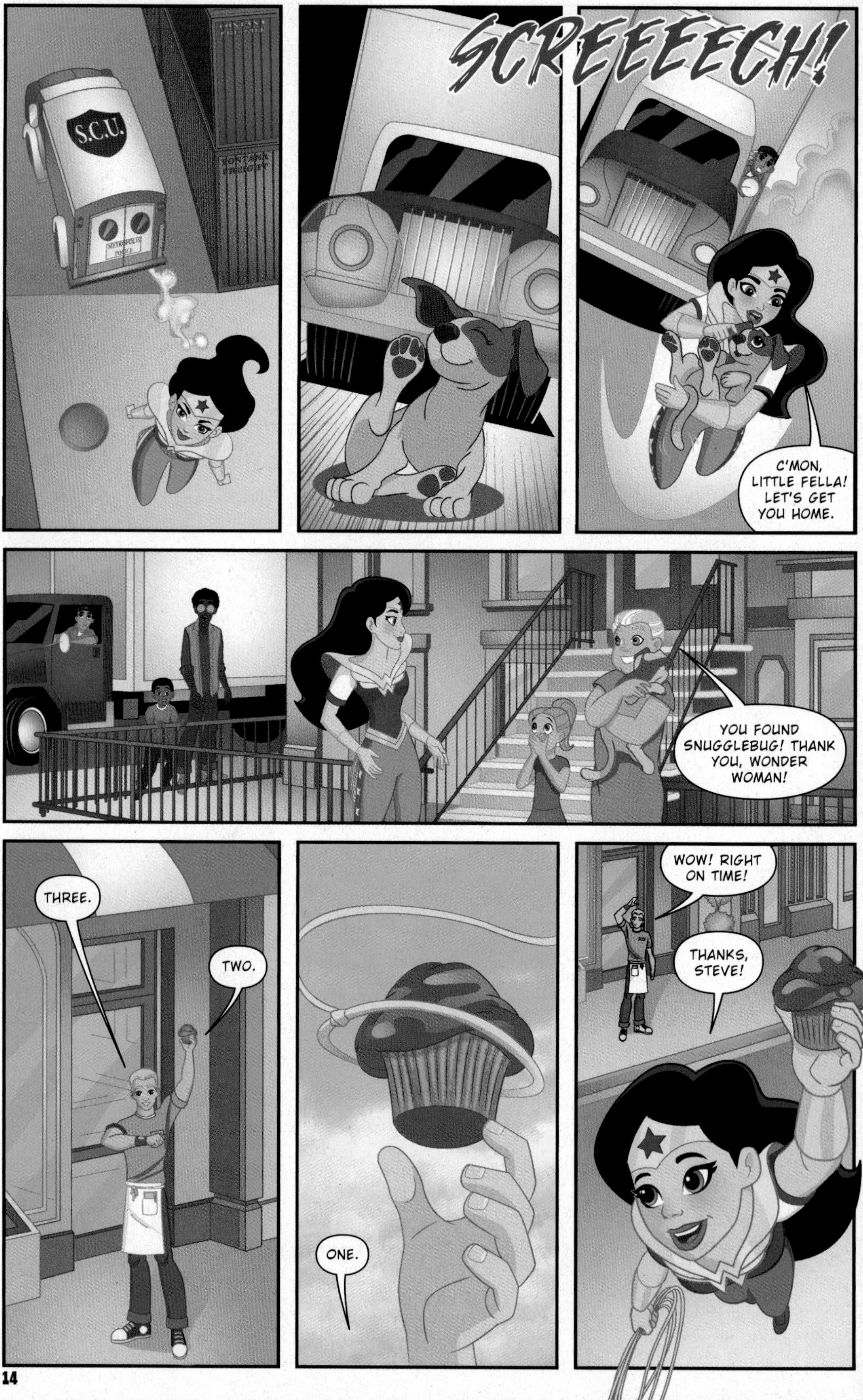
S.C.U.
SCREEEEECH!
C'MON, LITTLE FELLA! LET'S GET YOU HOME.
YOU FOUND SNUGGLEBUG! THANK YOU, WONDER WOMAN!
THREE.
TWO.
ONE.
WOW! RIGHT ON TIME!
THANKS, STEVE!

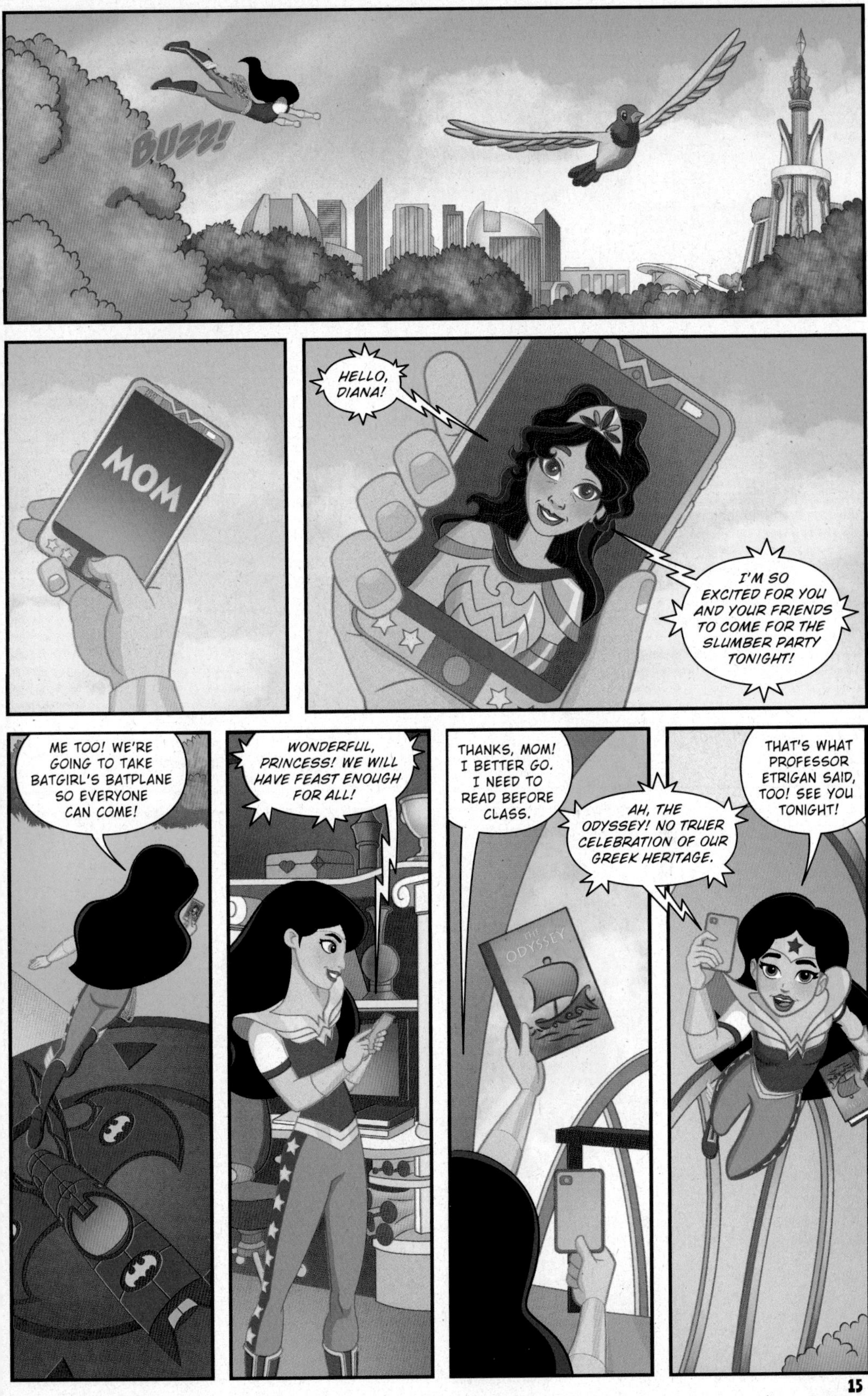

BUZZ!
MOM
HELLO, DIANA!
I'M SO EXCITED FOR YOU AND YOUR FRIENDS TO COME FOR THE SLUMBER PARTY TONIGHT!
ME TOO! WE'RE GOING TO TAKE BATGIRL'S BATPLANE SO EVERYONE CAN COME!
WONDERFUL, PRINCESS! WE WILL HAVE FEAST ENOUGH FOR ALL!
THANKS, MOM! I BETTER GO. I NEED TO READ BEFORE CLASS.
AH, THE ODYSSEY! NO TRUER CELEBRATION OF OUR GREEK HERITAGE.
THE ODYSSEY
THAT'S WHAT PROFESSOR ETRIGAN SAID, TOO! SEE YOU TONIGHT!

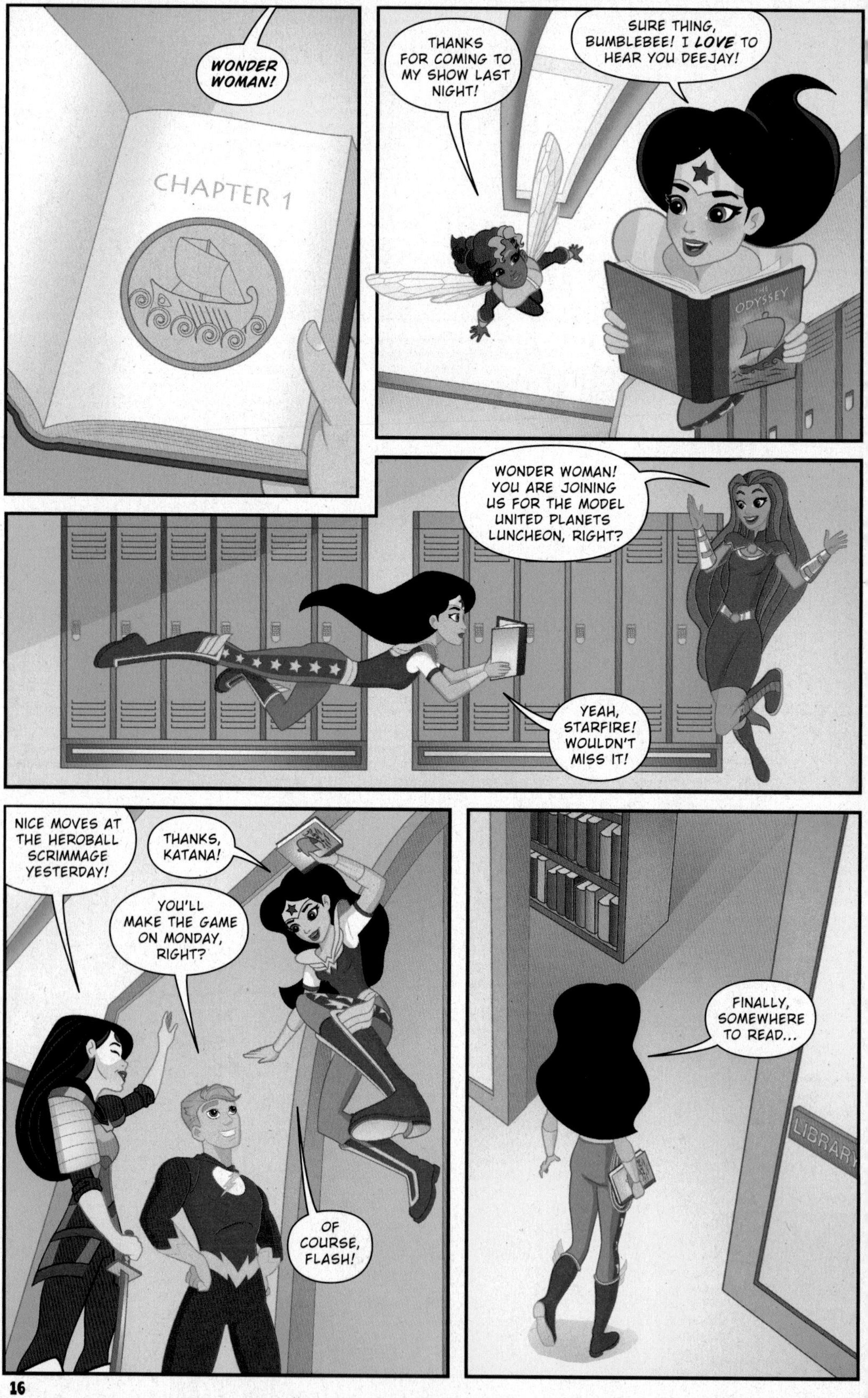
WONDER WOMAN!
CHAPTER 1
THANKS FOR COMING TO MY SHOW LAST NIGHT!
SURE THING, BUMBLEBEE! I LOVE TO HEAR YOU DEEJAY!
THE ODYSSEY
WONDER WOMAN! YOU ARE JOINING US FOR THE MODEL UNITED PLANETS LUNCHEON, RIGHT?
YEAH, STARFIRE! WOULDN'T MISS IT!
NICE MOVES AT THE HEROBALL SCRIMMAGE YESTERDAY!
THANKS, KATANA!
YOU'LL MAKE THE GAME ON MONDAY, RIGHT?
OF COURSE, FLASH!
FINALLY, SOMEWHERE TO READ...
LIBRARY

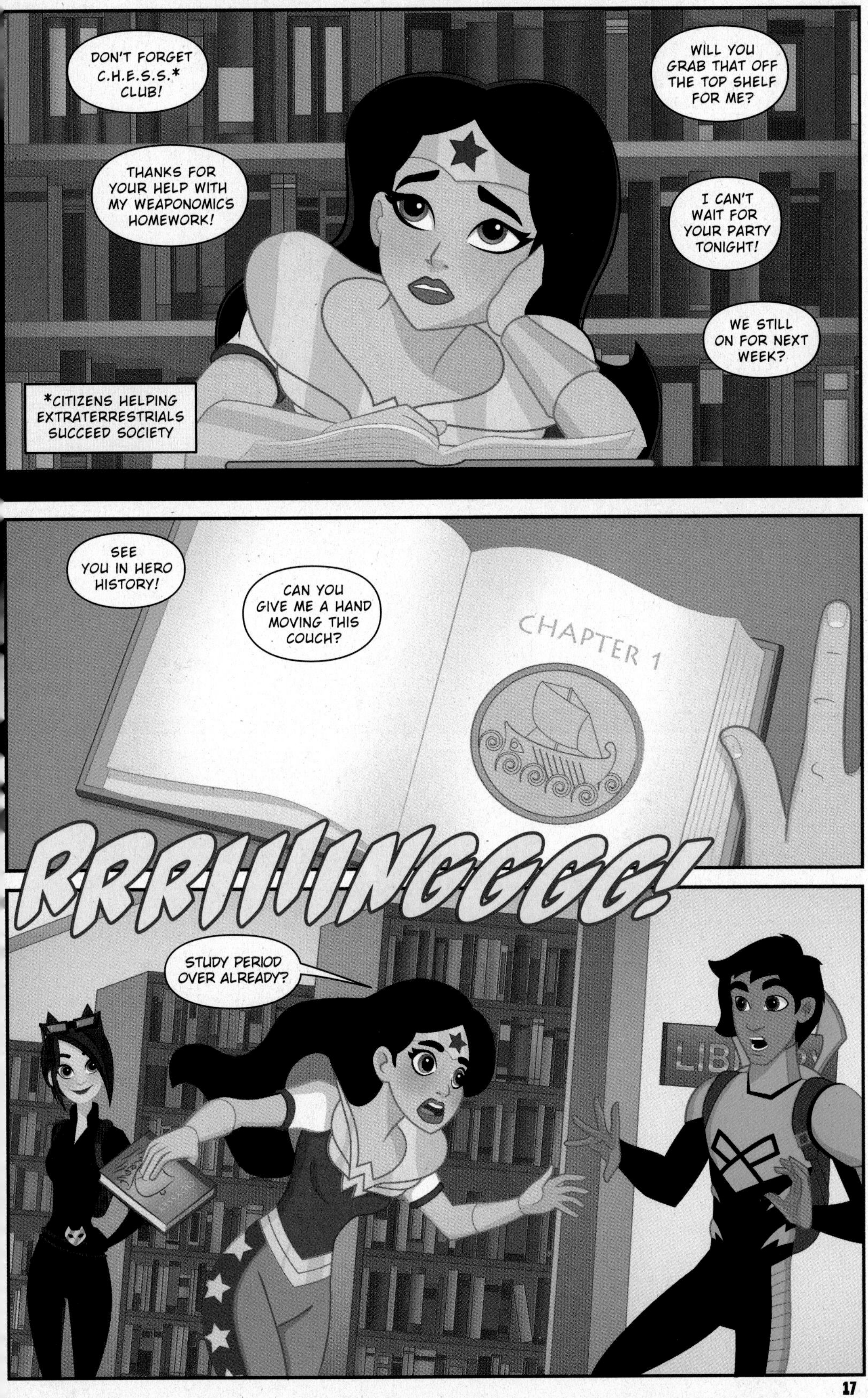
DON'T FORGET C.H.E.S.S.* CLUB!
WILL YOU GRAB THAT OFF THE TOP SHELF FOR ME?
THANKS FOR YOUR HELP WITH MY WEAPONOMICS HOMEWORK!
I CAN'T WAIT FOR YOUR PARTY TONIGHT!
WE STILL ON FOR NEXT WEEK?
*CITIZENS HELPING EXTRATERRESTRIALS SUCCEED SOCIETY
SEE YOU IN HERO HISTORY!
CAN YOU GIVE ME A HAND MOVING THIS COUCH?
CHAPTER 1
RRRIIIINGGGG!
STUDY PERIOD OVER ALREADY?

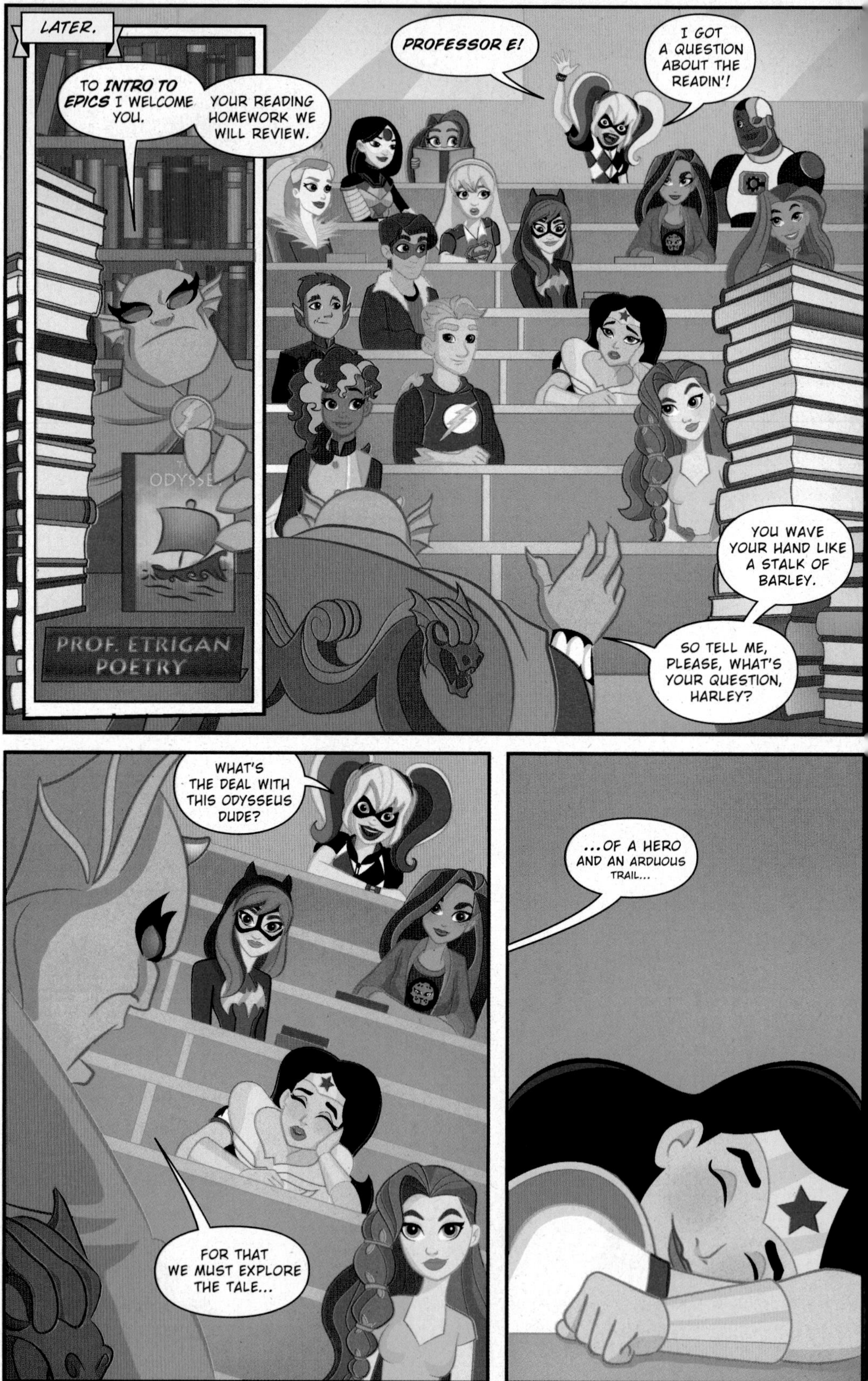
LATER.
TO INTRO TO EPICS I WELCOME YOU.
YOUR READING HOMEWORK WE WILL REVIEW.
PROFESSOR E!
I GOT A QUESTION ABOUT THE READIN'!
ODYSSE
PROF. ETRIGAN POETRY
YOU WAVE YOUR HAND LIKE A STALK OF BARLEY.
SO TELL ME, PLEASE, WHAT'S YOUR QUESTION, HARLEY?
WHAT'S THE DEAL WITH THIS ODYSSEUS DUDE?
FOR THAT WE MUST EXPLORE THE TALE...
...OF A HERO AND AN ARDUOUS TRAIL...

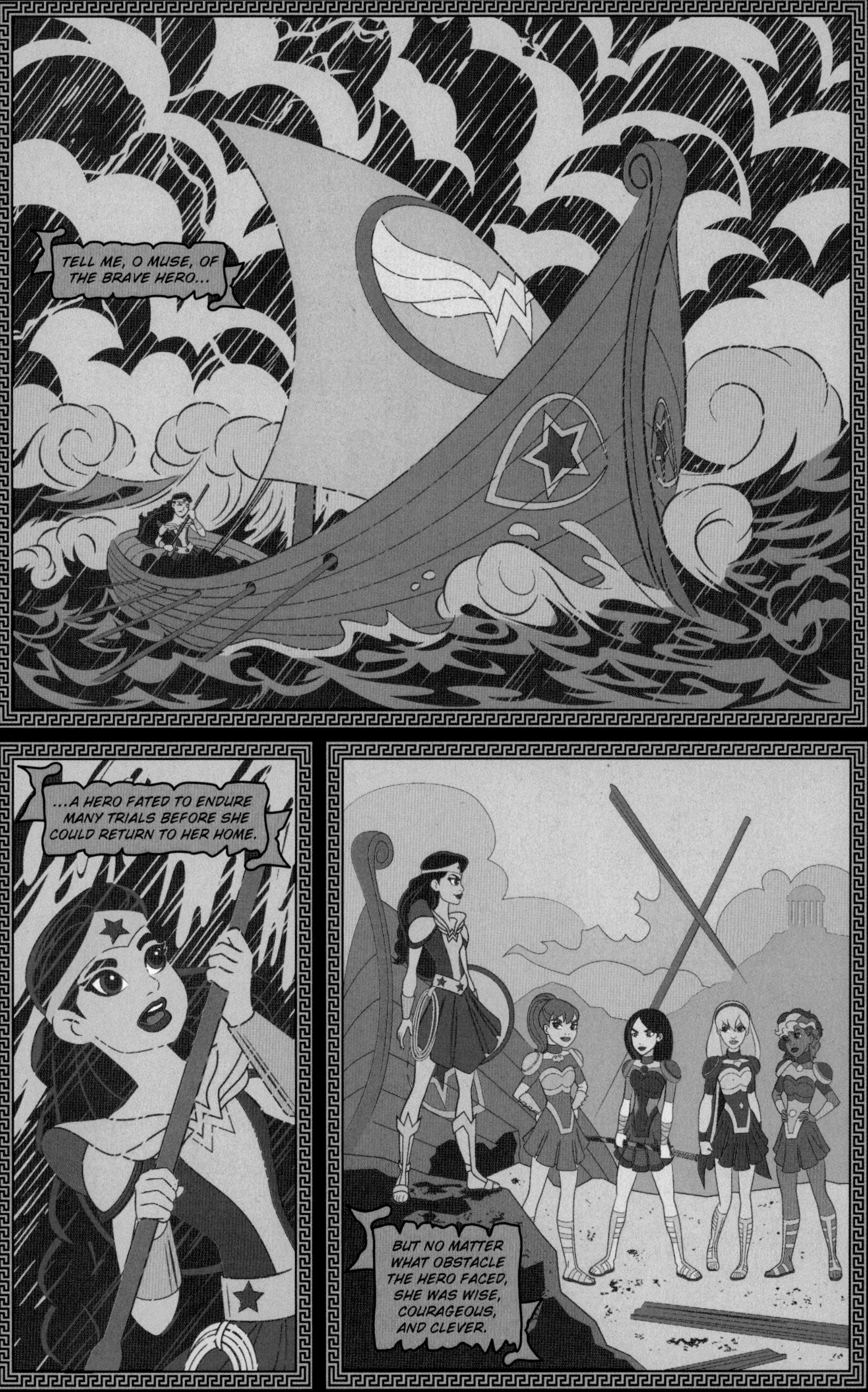
TELL ME, O MUSE, OF THE BRAVE HERO...
...A HERO FATED TO ENDURE MANY TRIALS BEFORE SHE COULD RETURN TO HER HOME.
BUT NO MATTER WHAT OBSTACLE THE HERO FACED, SHE WAS WISE, COURAGEOUS, AND CLEVER.

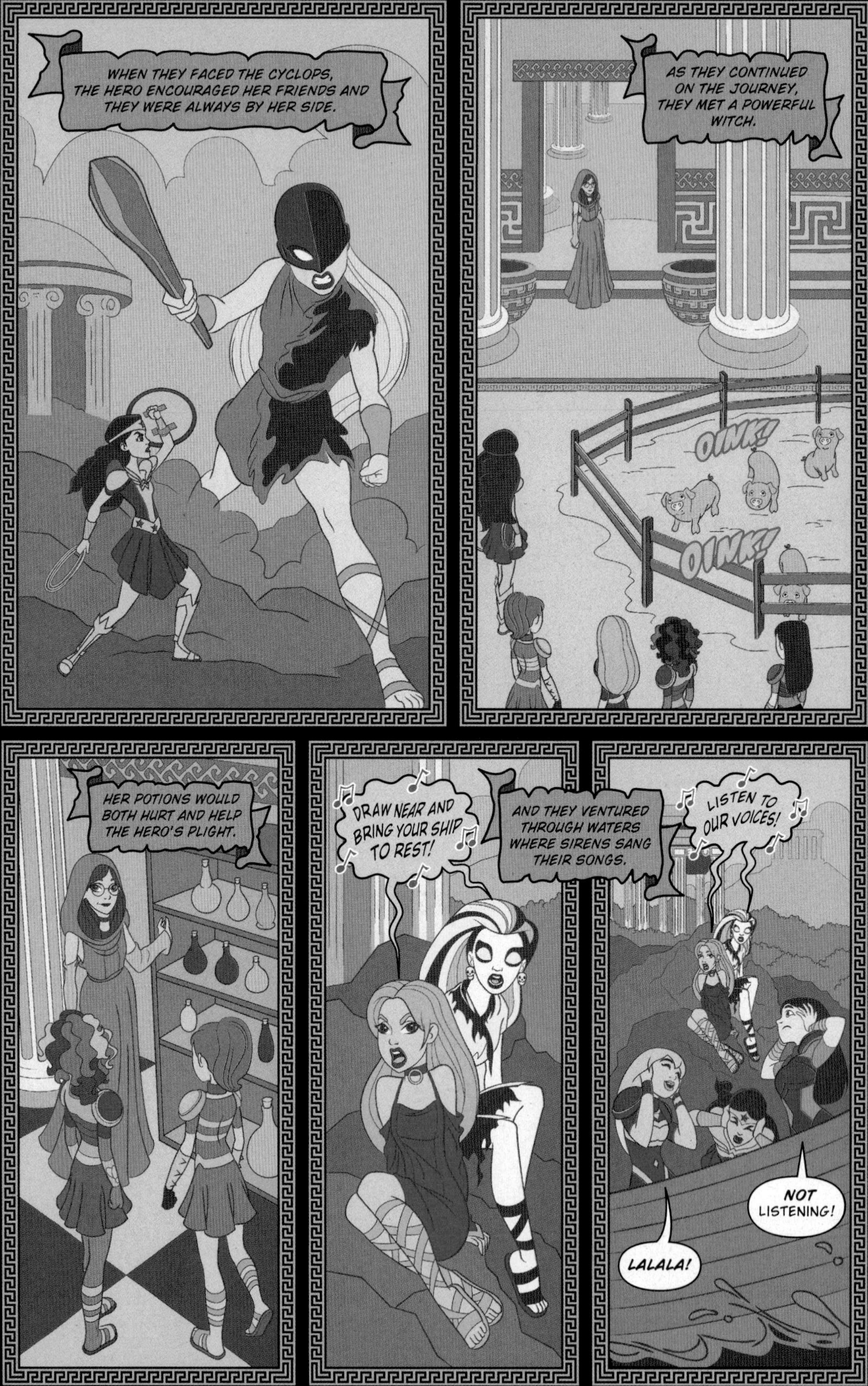
WHEN THEY FACED THE CYCLOPS, THE HERO ENCOURAGED HER FRIENDS AND THEY WERE ALWAYS BY HER SIDE.
AS THEY CONTINUED ON THE JOURNEY, THEY MET A POWERFUL WITCH.
OINK!
OINK!
HER POTIONS WOULD BOTH HURT AND HELP THE HERO'S PLIGHT.
DRAW NEAR AND BRING YOUR SHIP TO REST!
AND THEY VENTURED THROUGH WATERS WHERE SIRENS SANG THEIR SONGS.
LISTEN TO OUR VOICES!
NOT LISTENING!
LALALA!

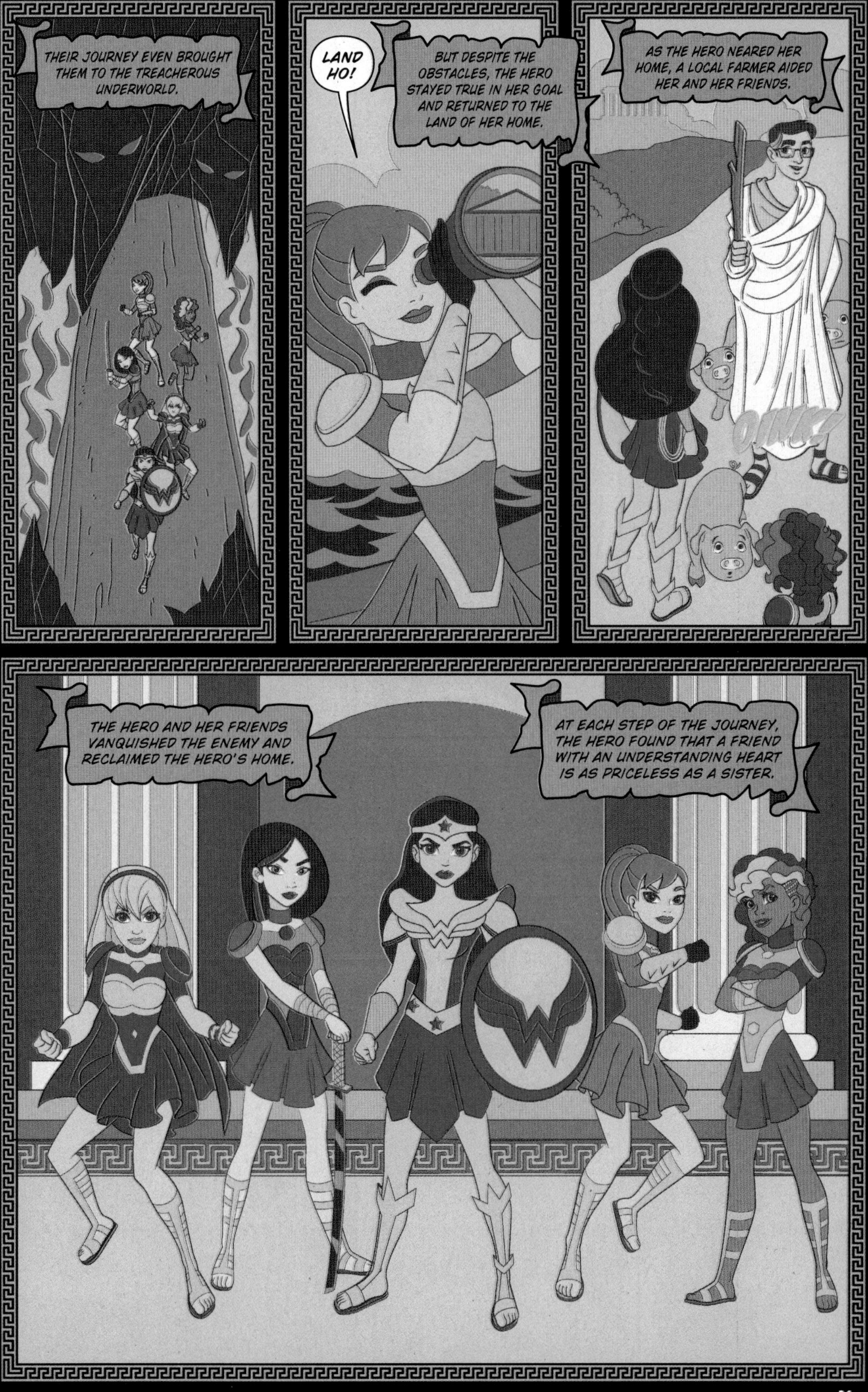
THEIR JOURNEY EVEN BROUGHT THEM TO THE TREACHEROUS UNDERWORLD.
LAND HO!
BUT DESPITE THE OBSTACLES, THE HERO STAYED TRUE IN HER GOAL AND RETURNED TO THE LAND OF HER HOME.
AS THE HERO NEARED HER HOME, A LOCAL FARMER AIDED HER AND HER FRIENDS.
OINK!
THE HERO AND HER FRIENDS VANQUISHED THE ENEMY AND RECLAIMED THE HERO'S HOME.
AT EACH STEP OF THE JOURNEY, THE HERO FOUND THAT A FRIEND WITH AN UNDERSTANDING HEART IS AS PRICELESS AS A SISTER.

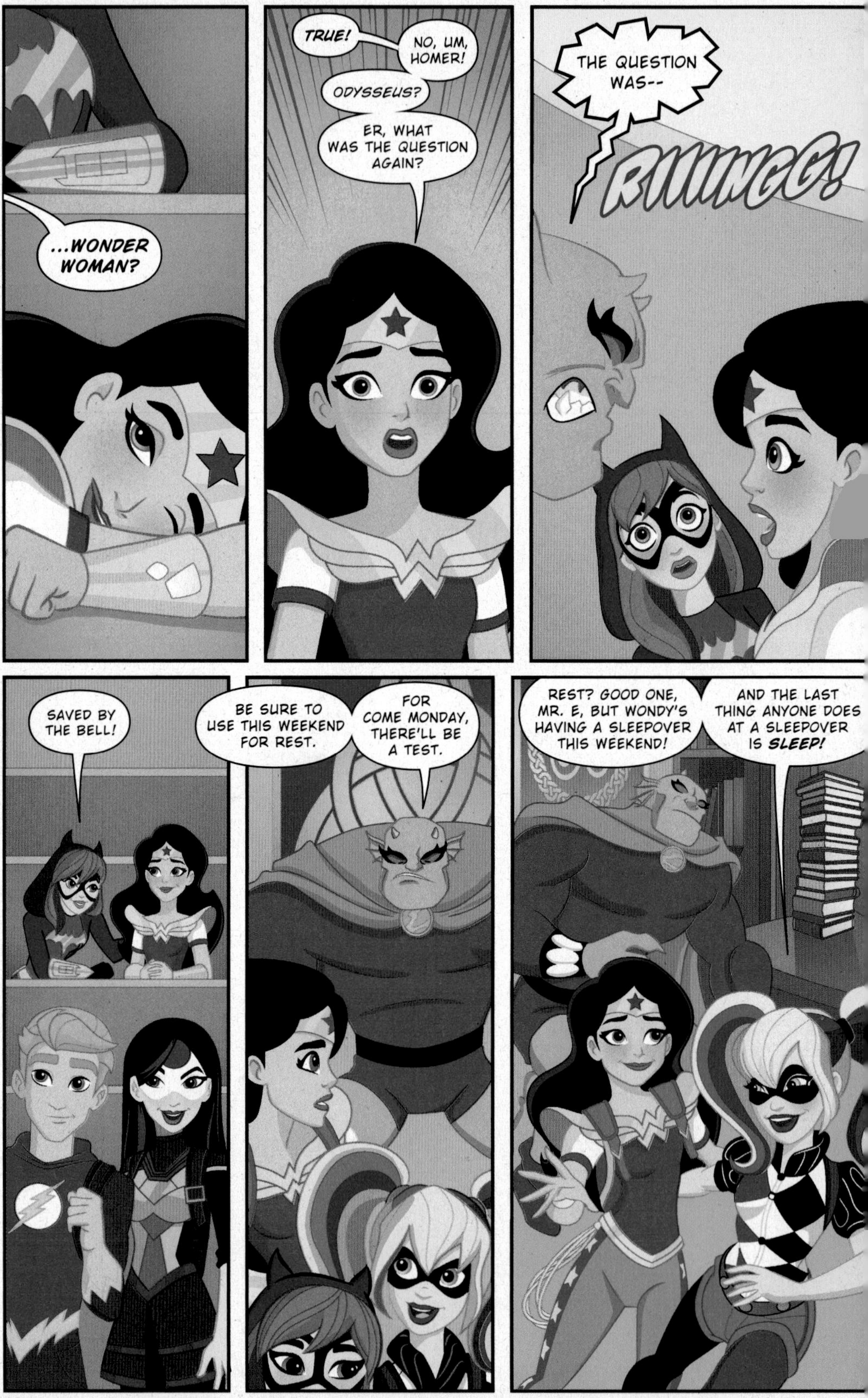
...WONDER WOMAN?
TRUE!
NO, UM, HOMER!
ODYSSEUS?
ER, WHAT WAS THE QUESTION AGAIN?
THE QUESTION WAS--
RIIIINGG!
SAVED BY THE BELL!
BE SURE TO USE THIS WEEKEND FOR REST.
FOR COME MONDAY, THERE'LL BE A TEST.
REST? GOOD ONE, MR. E, BUT WONDY'S HAVING A SLEEPOVER THIS WEEKEND!
AND THE LAST THING ANYONE DOES AT A SLEEPOVER IS SLEEP!

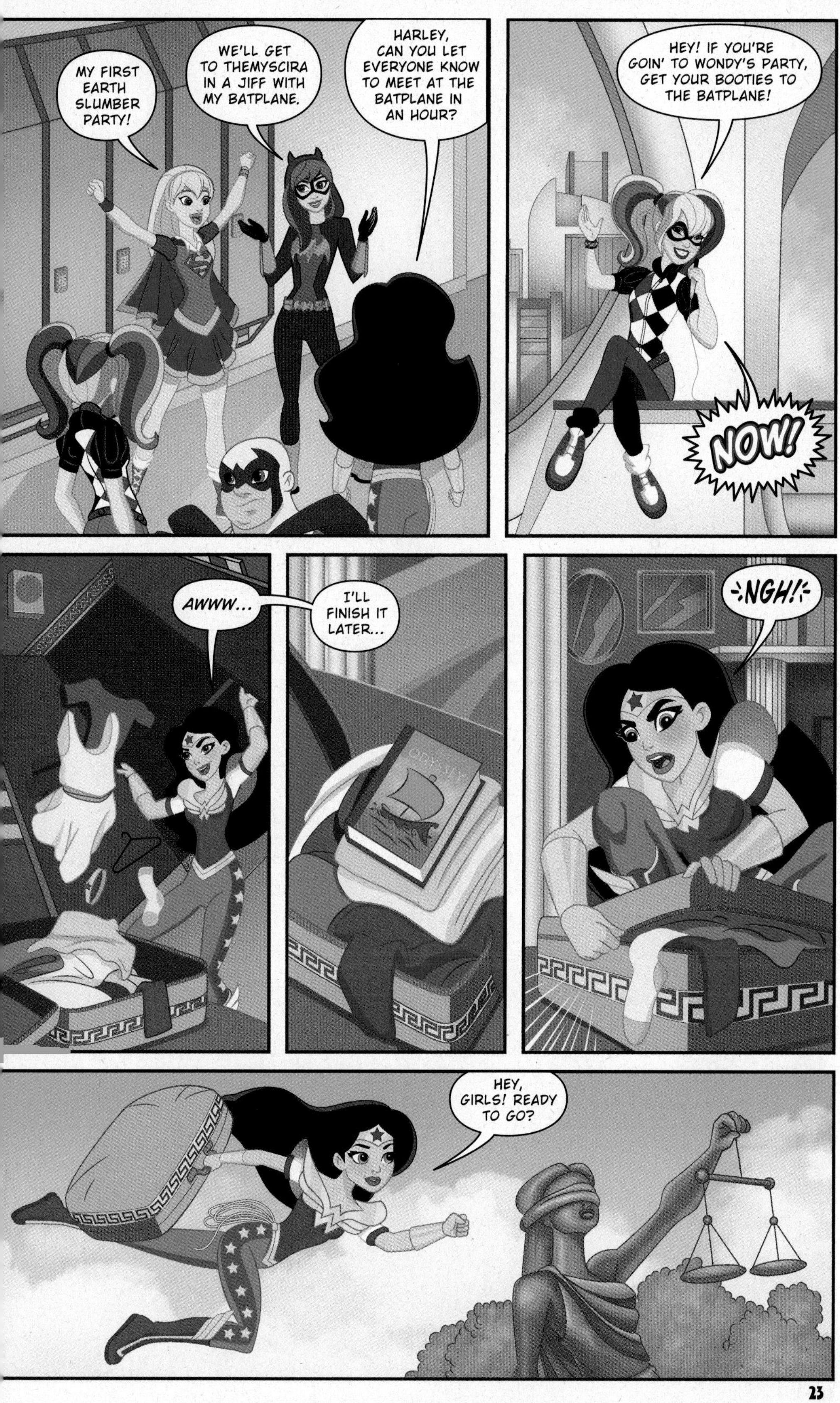
MY FIRST EARTH SLUMBER PARTY!
WE'LL GET TO THEMYSCIRA IN A JIFF WITH MY BATPLANE.
HARLEY, CAN YOU LET EVERYONE KNOW TO MEET AT THE BATPLANE IN AN HOUR?
HEY! IF YOU'RE GOIN' TO WONDY'S PARTY, GET YOUR BOOTIES TO THE BATPLANE!
NOW!
AWWW...
I'LL FINISH IT LATER...
THE ODYSSEY
NGH!
HEY, GIRLS! READY TO GO?

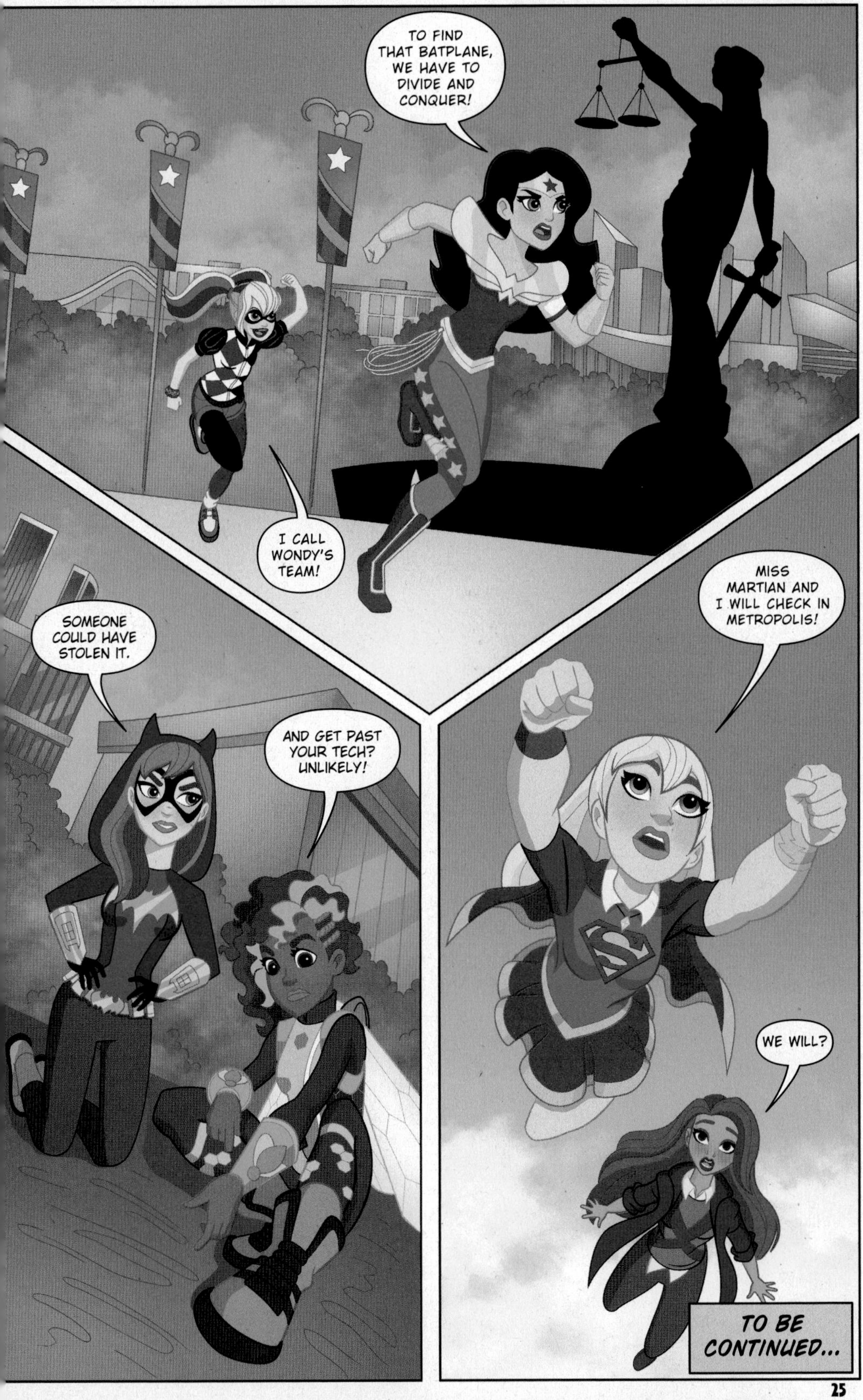
TO FIND THAT BATPLANE, WE HAVE TO DIVIDE AND CONQUER!
I CALL WONDY'S TEAM!
SOMEONE COULD HAVE STOLEN IT.
AND GET PAST YOUR TECH? UNLIKELY!
MISS MARTIAN AND I WILL CHECK IN METROPOLIS!
WE WILL?
TO BE CONTINUED...

CHAPTER TWO
THE CYCLOPS

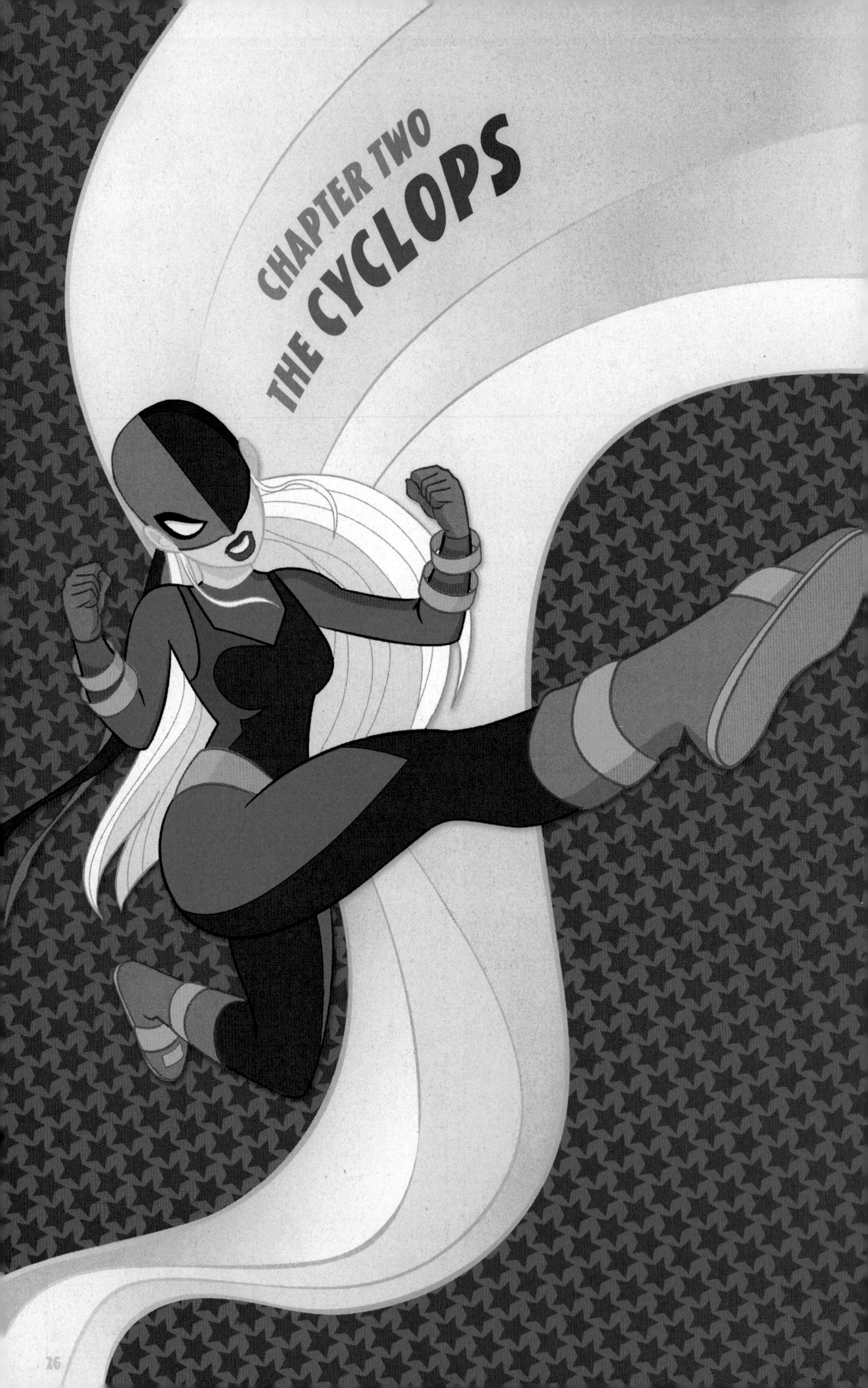

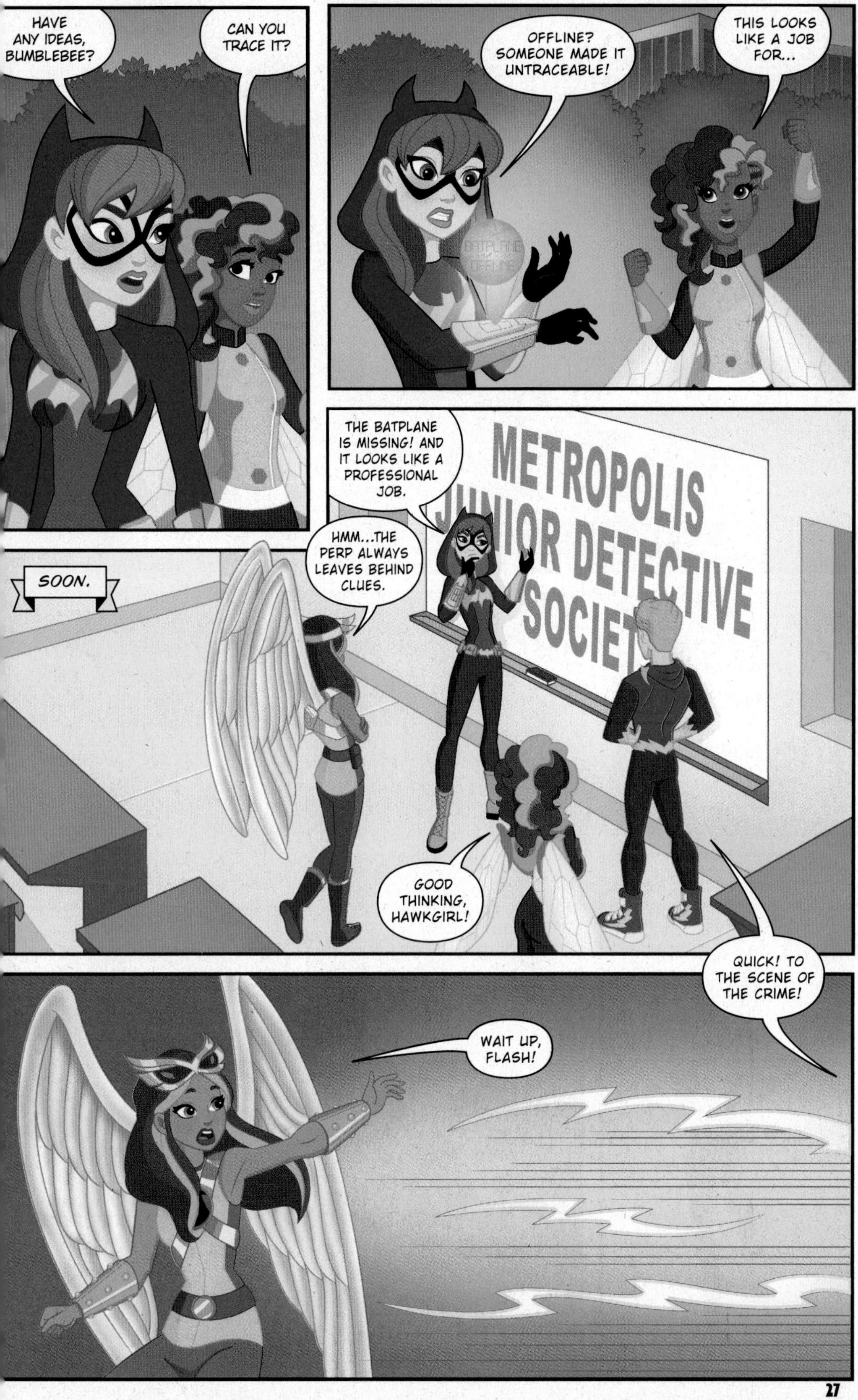

HAVE ANY IDEAS, BUMBLEBEE?
CAN YOU TRACE IT?
OFFLINE? SOMEONE MADE IT UNTRACEABLE!
BATPLANE OFFLINE
THIS LOOKS LIKE A JOB FOR...
SOON.
METROPOLIS JUNIOR DETECTIVE SOCIET
THE BATPLANE IS MISSING! AND IT LOOKS LIKE A PROFESSIONAL JOB.
HMM...THE PERP ALWAYS LEAVES BEHIND CLUES.
GOOD THINKING, HAWKGIRL!
QUICK! TO THE SCENE OF THE CRIME!
WAIT UP, FLASH!

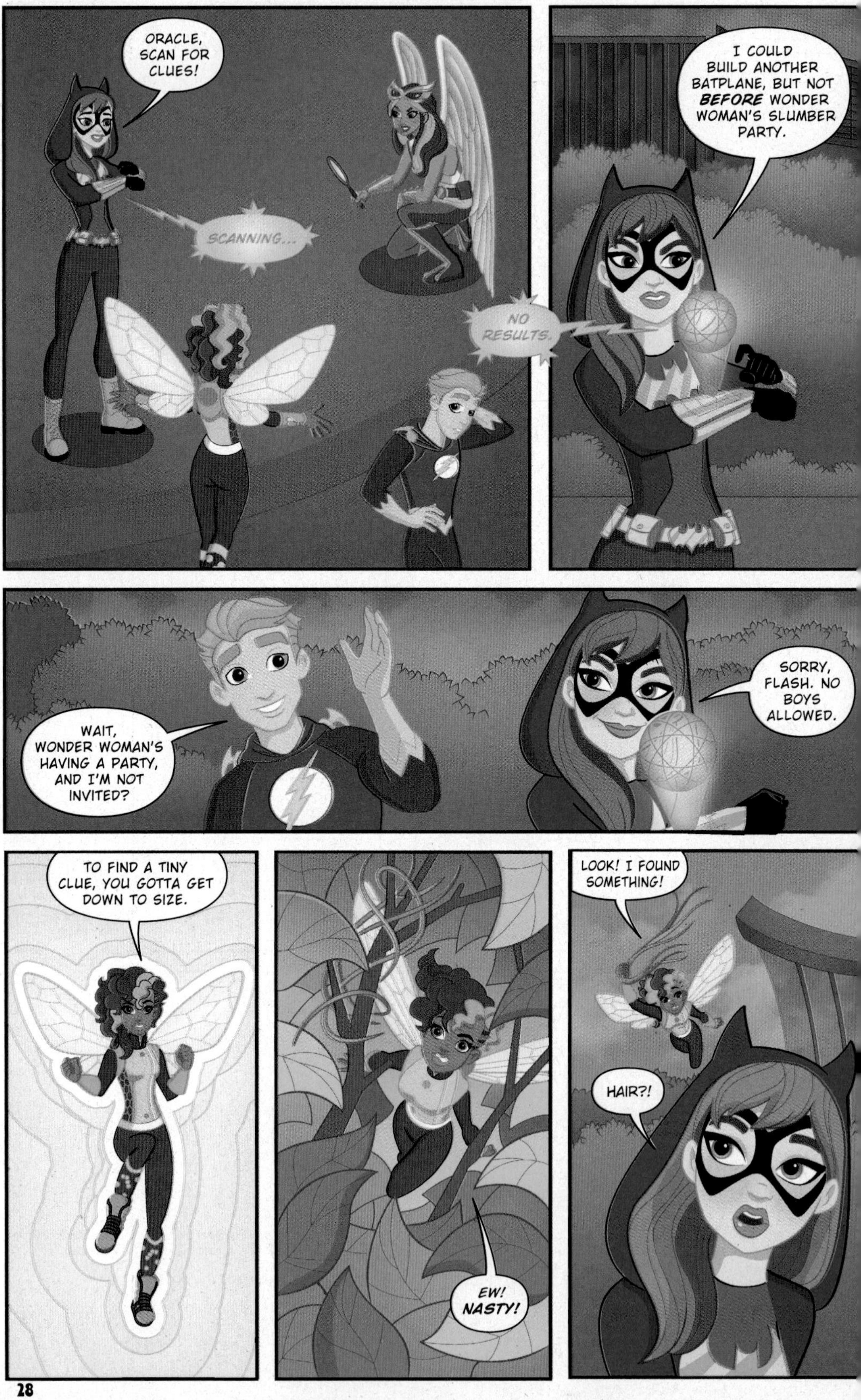
ORACLE, SCAN FOR CLUES!
SCANNING...
NO RESULTS.
I COULD BUILD ANOTHER BATPLANE, BUT NOT *BEFORE* WONDER WOMAN'S SLUMBER PARTY.
WAIT, WONDER WOMAN'S HAVING A PARTY, AND I'M NOT INVITED?
SORRY, FLASH. NO BOYS ALLOWED.
TO FIND A TINY CLUE, YOU GOTTA GET DOWN TO SIZE.
EW! **NASTY!**
LOOK! I FOUND SOMETHING!
HAIR?!

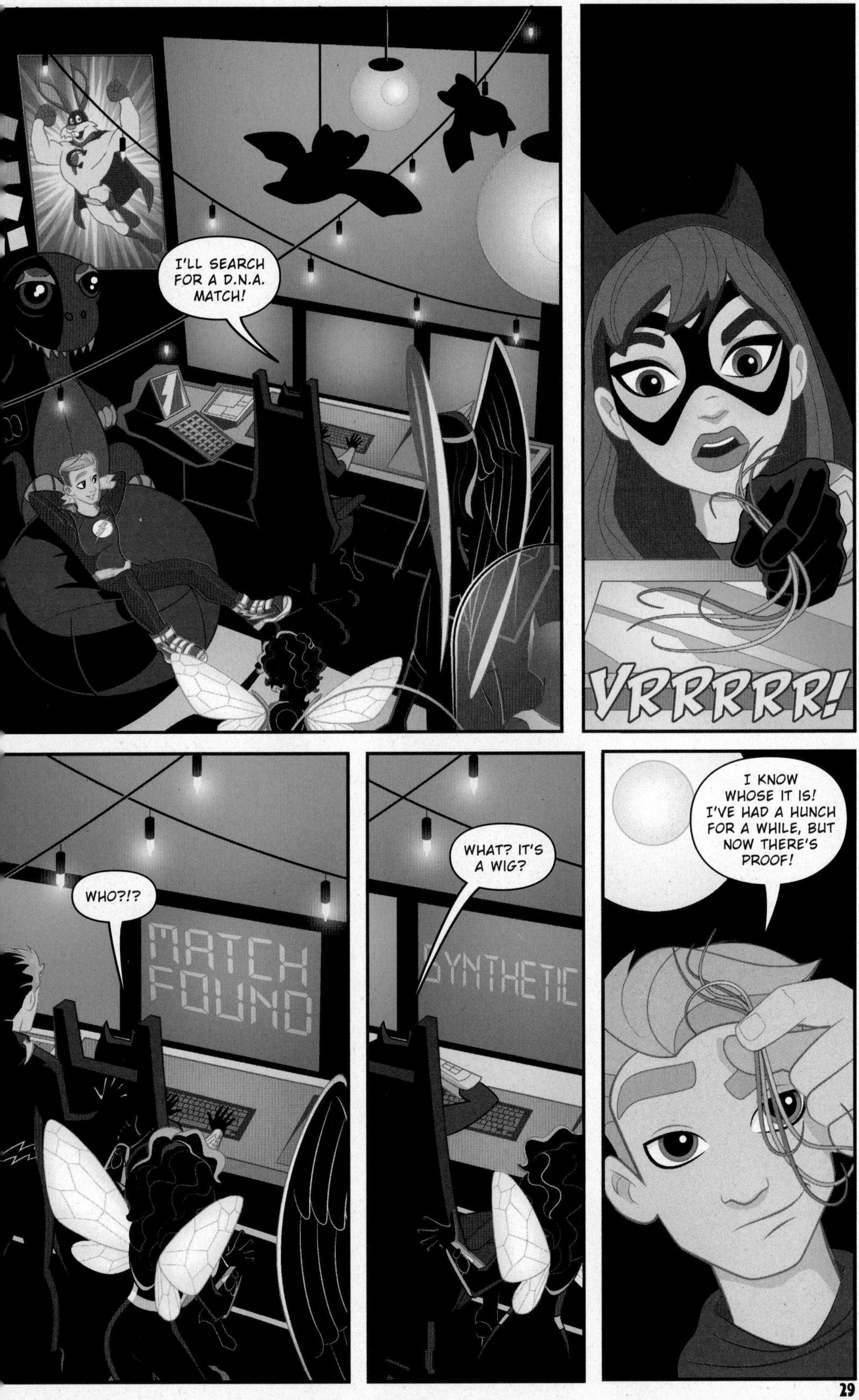

I'LL SEARCH FOR A D.N.A. MATCH!
VRRRRR!
WHO?!?
MATCH FOUND
WHAT? IT'S A WIG?
SYNTHETIC
I KNOW WHOSE IT IS! I'VE HAD A HUNCH FOR A WHILE, BUT NOW THERE'S PROOF!

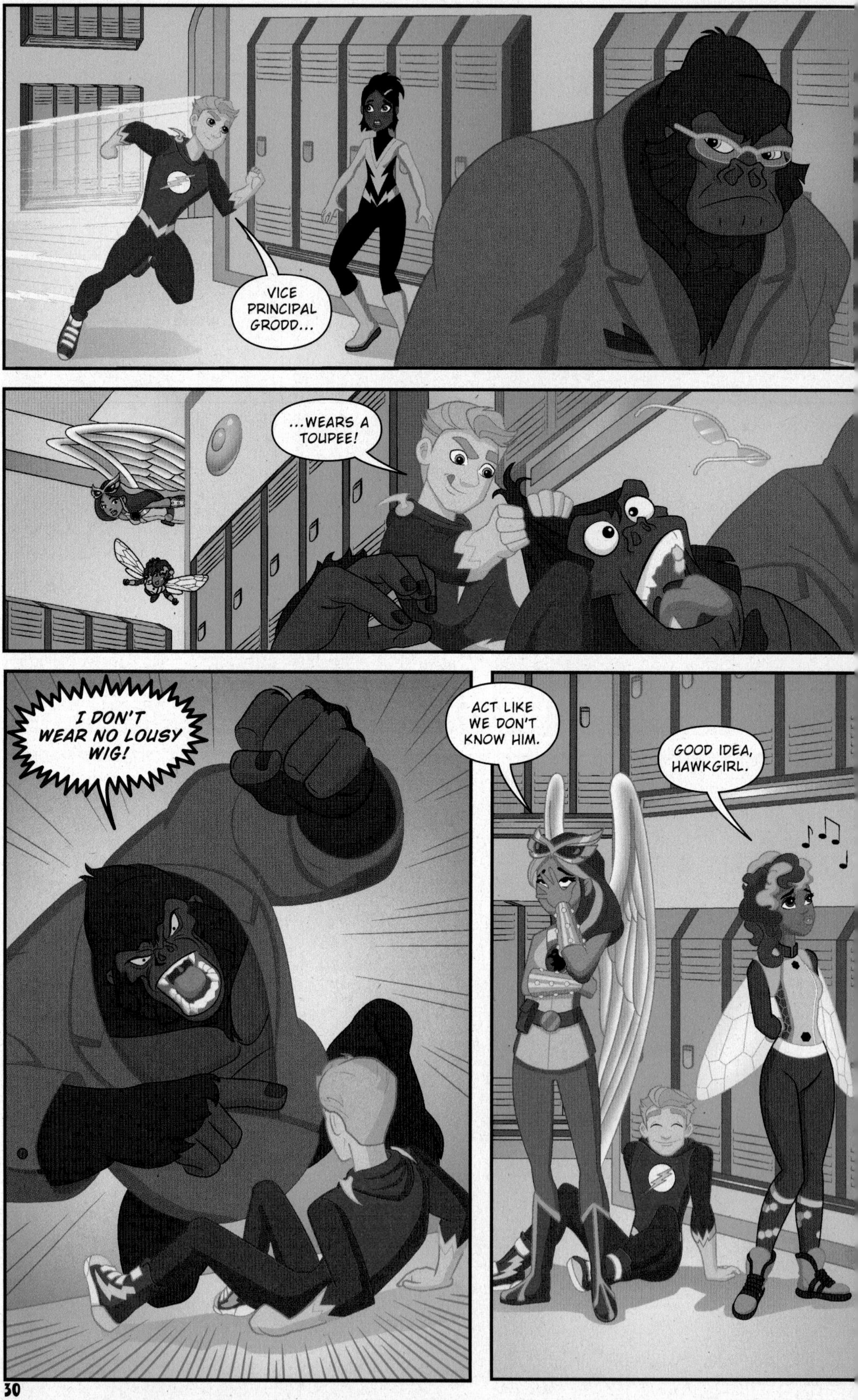

VICE PRINCIPAL GRODD...
...WEARS A TOUPEE!
I DON'T WEAR NO LOUSY WIG!
ACT LIKE WE DON'T KNOW HIM.
GOOD IDEA, HAWKGIRL.

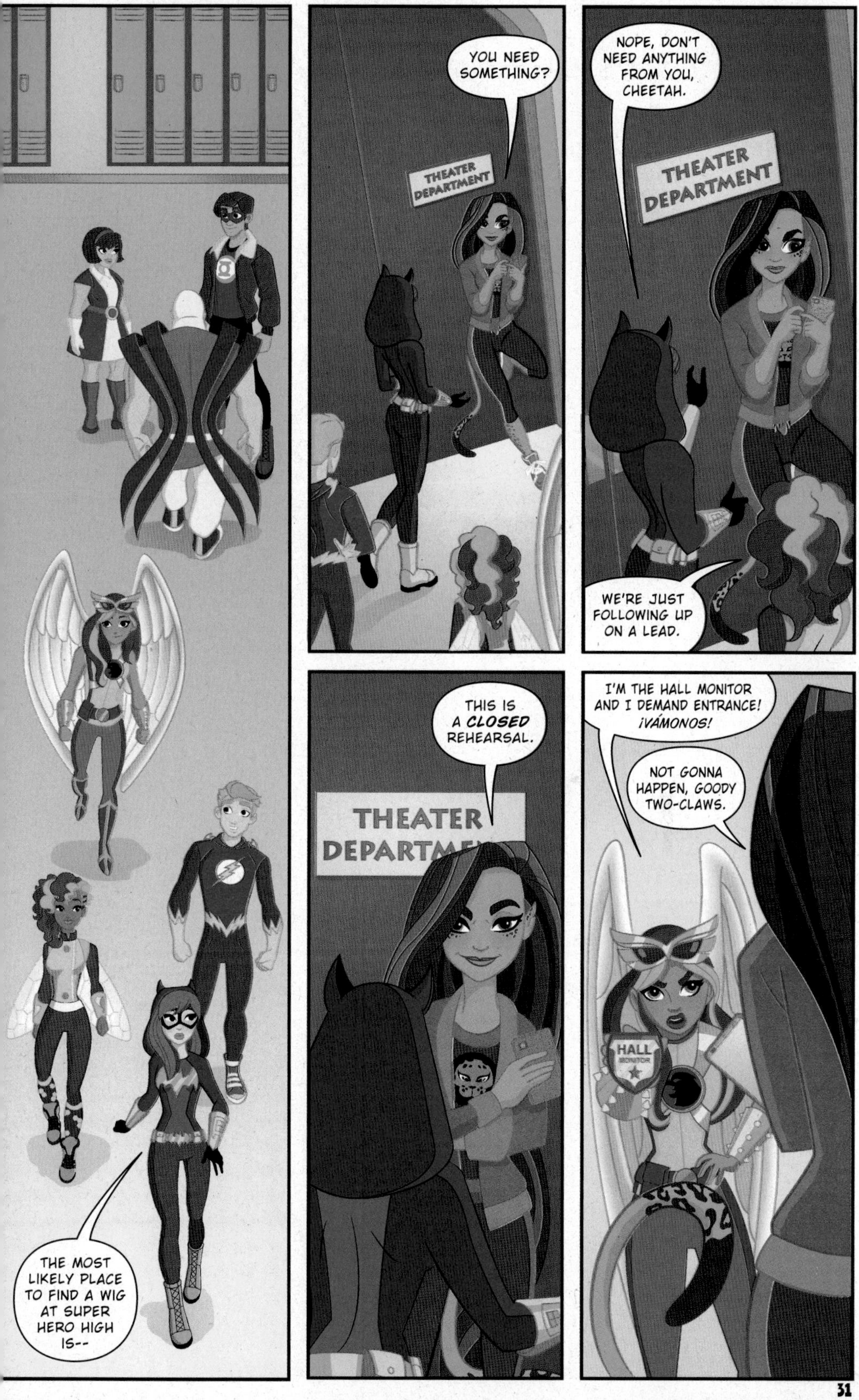

THE MOST LIKELY PLACE TO FIND A WIG AT SUPER HERO HIGH IS--
YOU NEED SOMETHING?
THEATER DEPARTMENT
NOPE, DON'T NEED ANYTHING FROM YOU, CHEETAH.
THEATER DEPARTMENT
WE'RE JUST FOLLOWING UP ON A LEAD.
THIS IS A ***CLOSED*** REHEARSAL.
THEATER DEPARTM
I'M THE HALL MONITOR AND I DEMAND ENTRANCE! *¡VÁMONOS!*
NOT GONNA HAPPEN, GOODY TWO-CLAWS.
HALL MONITOR

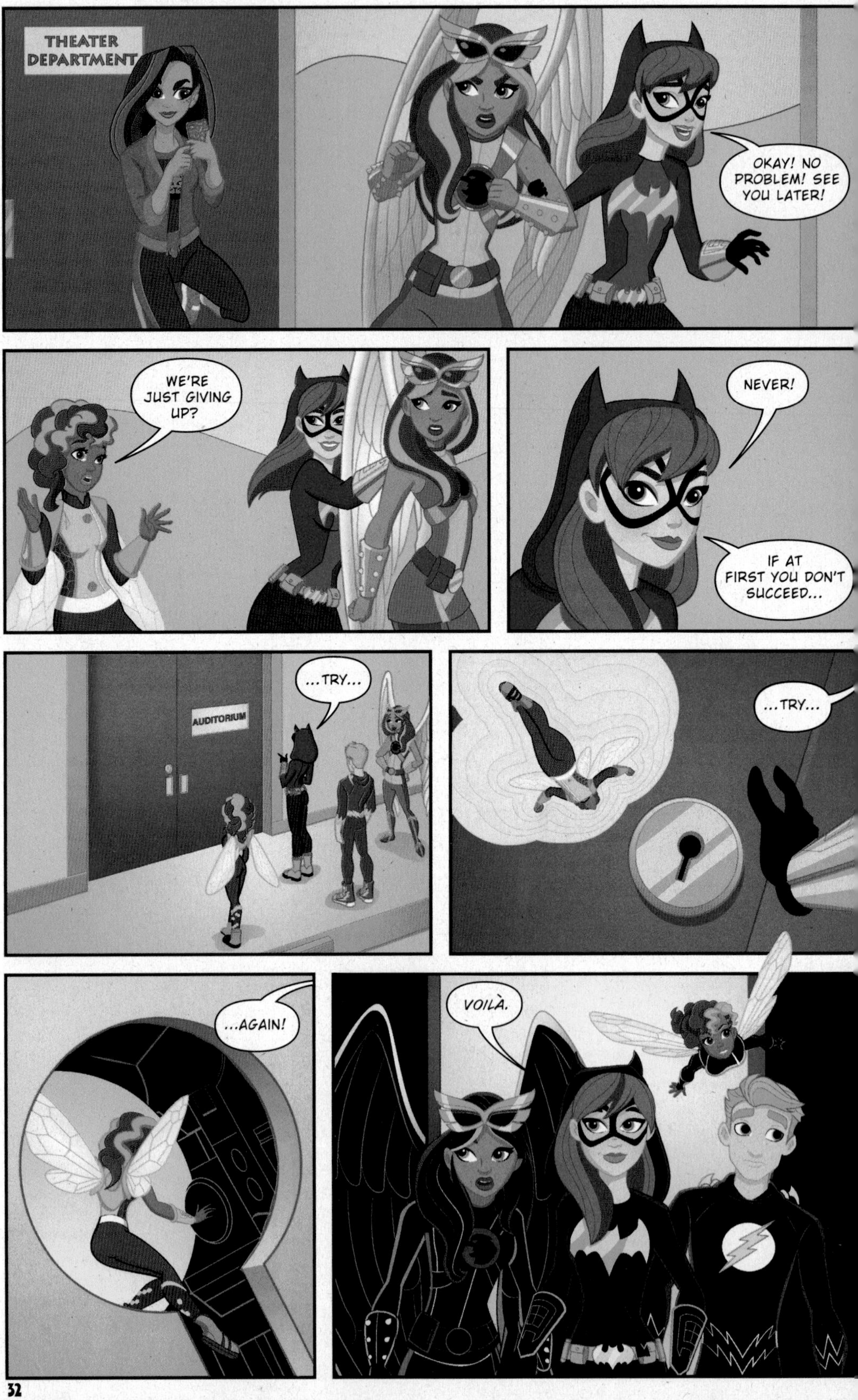
THEATER DEPARTMENT
OKAY! NO PROBLEM! SEE YOU LATER!
WE'RE JUST GIVING UP?
NEVER!
IF AT FIRST YOU DON'T SUCCEED...
AUDITORIUM
...TRY...
...TRY...
...AGAIN!
VOILÀ.

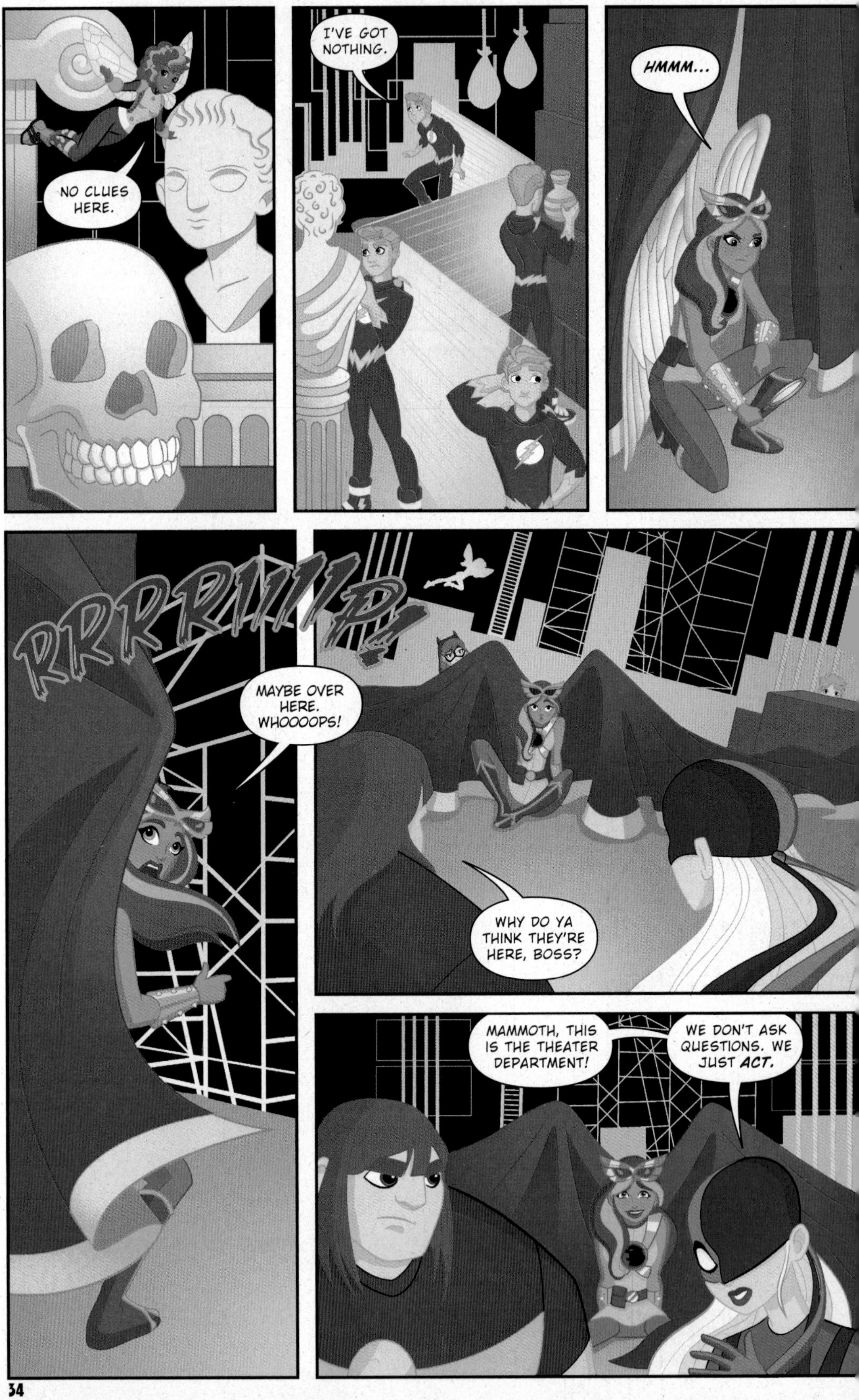
NO CLUES HERE.
I'VE GOT NOTHING.
HMMM...
RRRRIIIIP!
MAYBE OVER HERE. WHOOOOPS!
WHY DO YA THINK THEY'RE HERE, BOSS?
MAMMOTH, THIS IS THE THEATER DEPARTMENT!
WE DON'T ASK QUESTIONS. WE JUST ***ACT***.

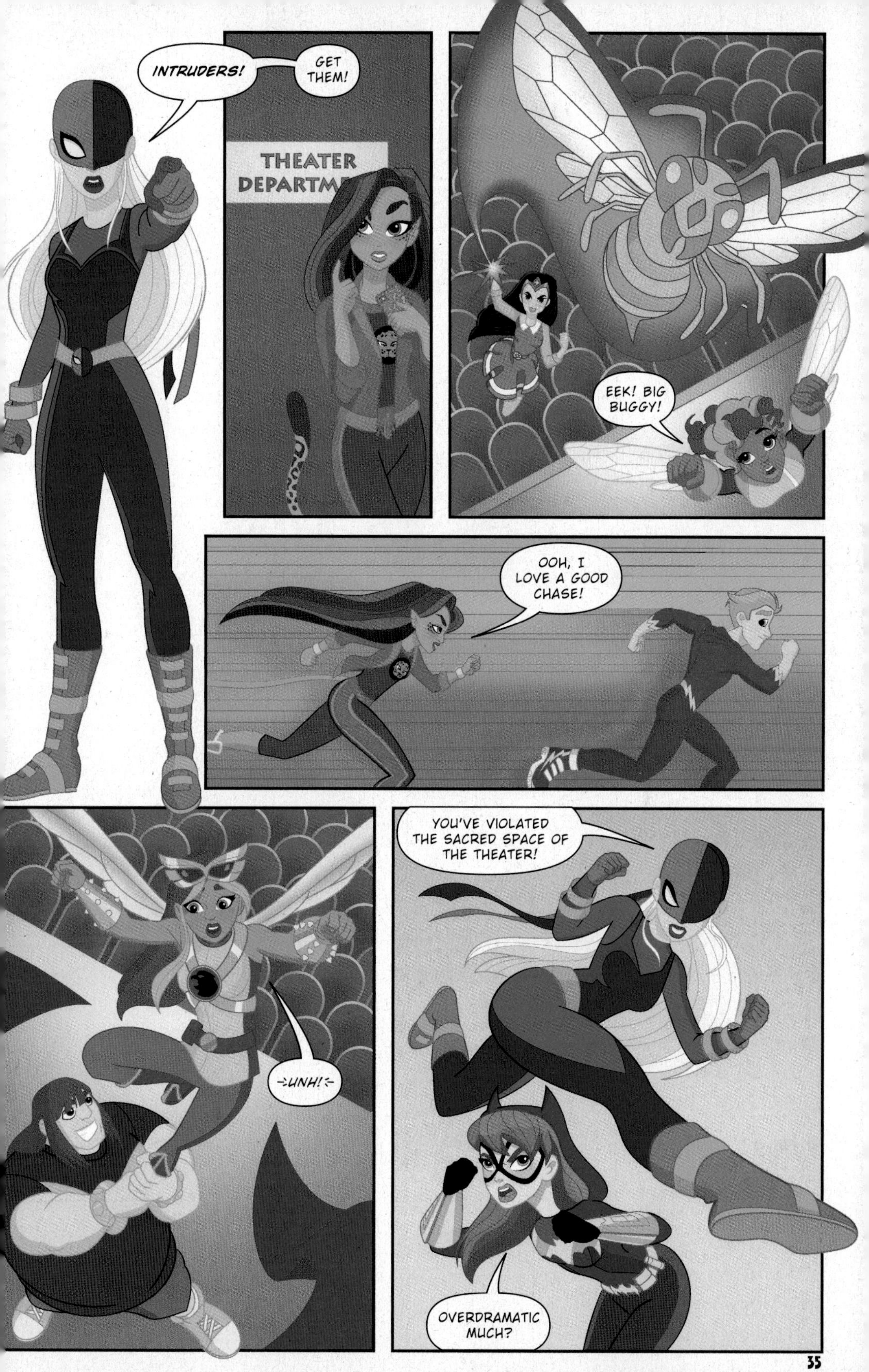
INTRUDERS!
GET THEM!
THEATER DEPARTM
EEK! BIG BUGGY!
OOH, I LOVE A GOOD CHASE!
UNH!
YOU'VE VIOLATED THE SACRED SPACE OF THE THEATER!
OVERDRAMATIC MUCH?

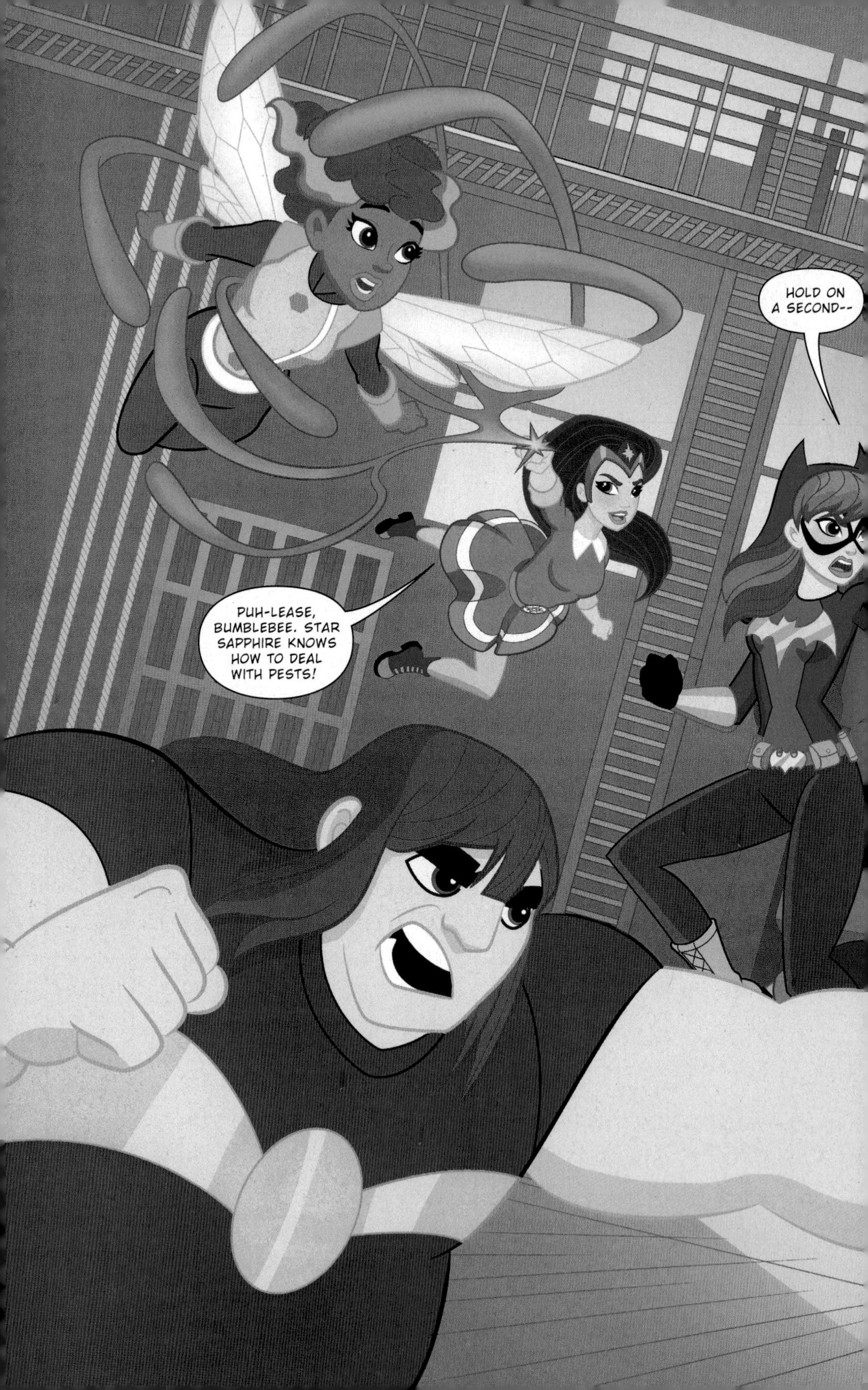
HOLD ON A SECOND--
PUH-LEASE, BUMBLEBEE. STAR SAPPHIRE KNOWS HOW TO DEAL WITH PESTS!

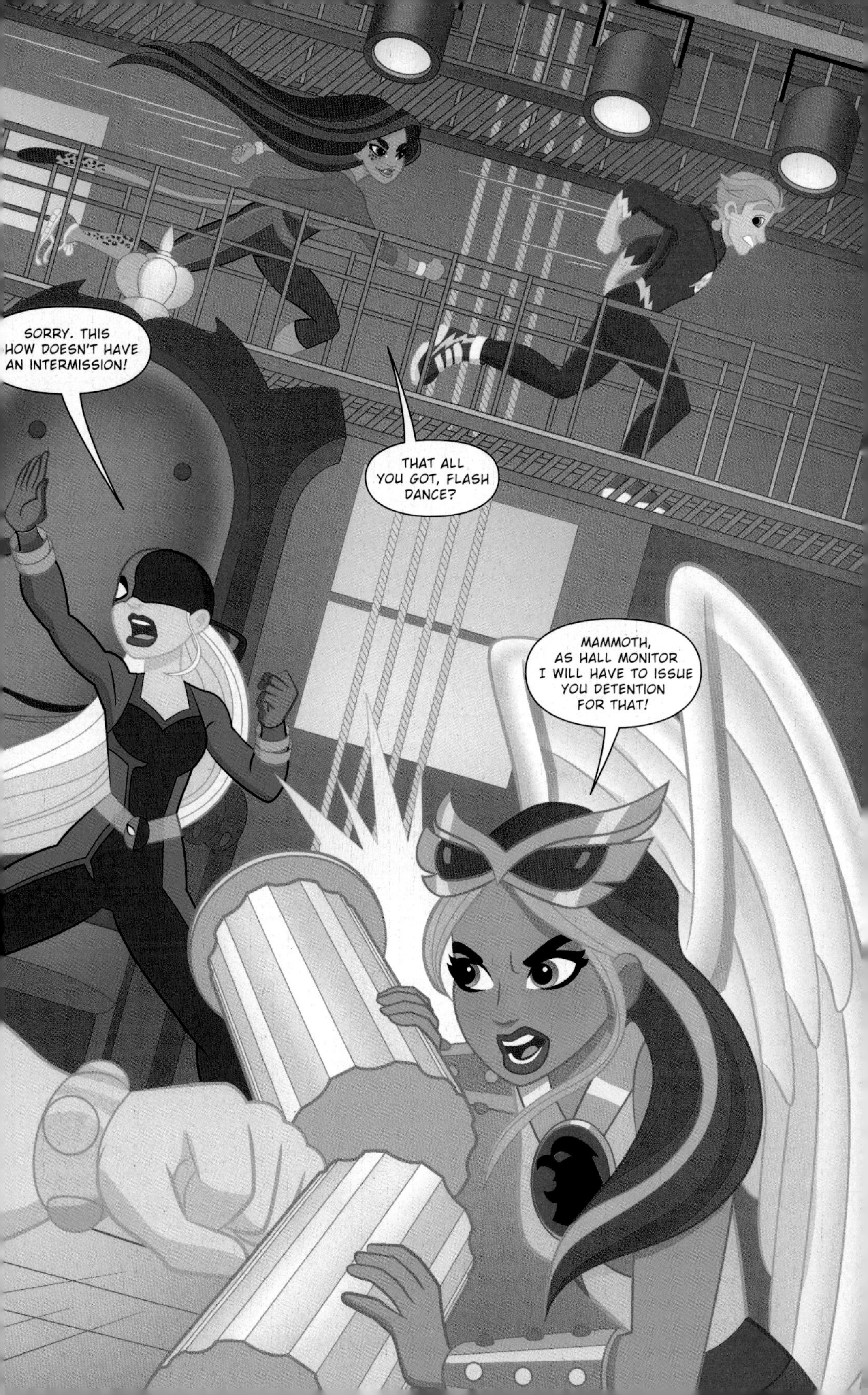
SORRY. THIS HOW DOESN'T HAVE AN INTERMISSION!
THAT ALL YOU GOT, FLASH DANCE?
MAMMOTH, AS HALL MONITOR I WILL HAVE TO ISSUE YOU DETENTION FOR THAT!

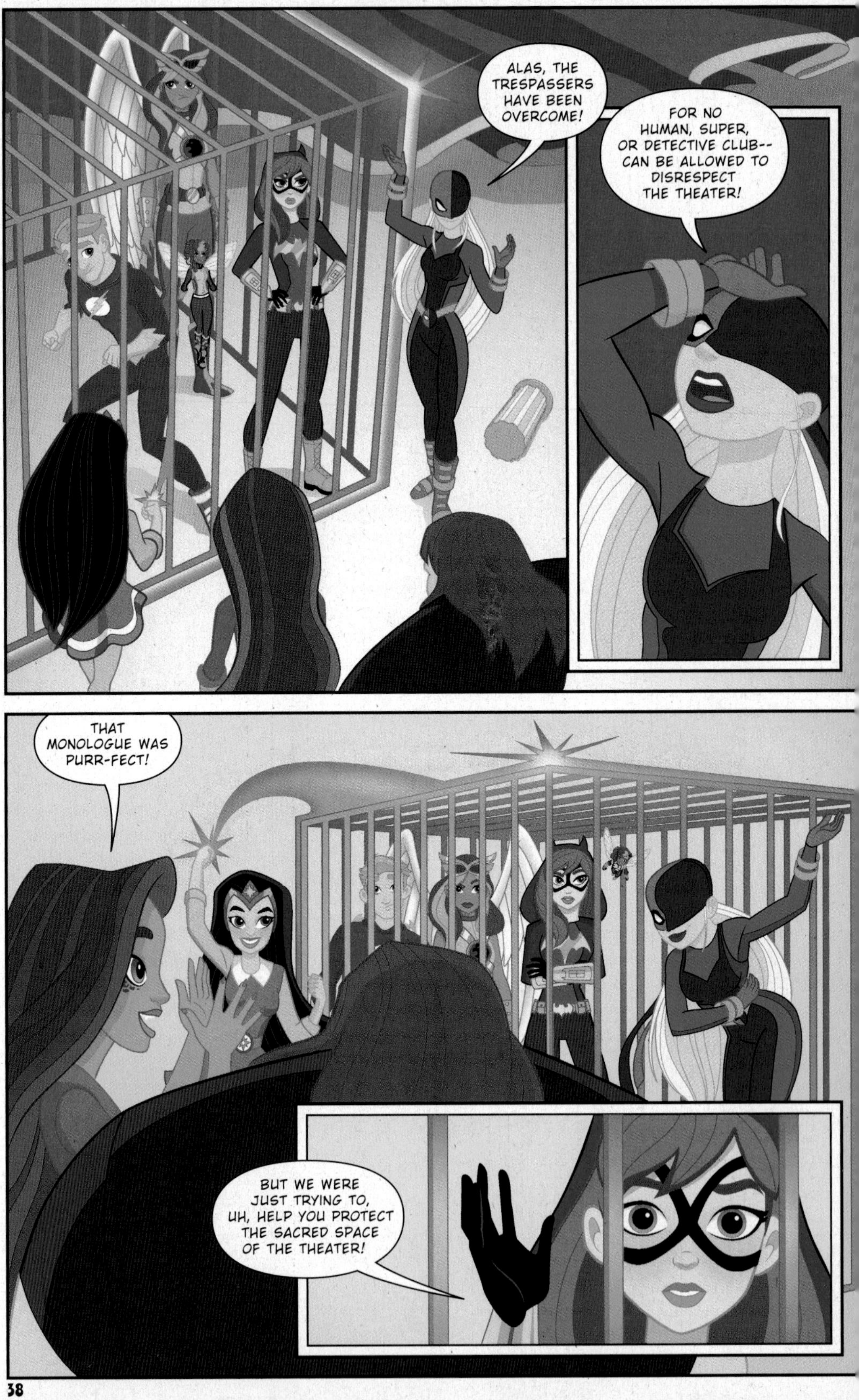
ALAS, THE TRESPASSERS HAVE BEEN OVERCOME!
FOR NO HUMAN, SUPER, OR DETECTIVE CLUB-- CAN BE ALLOWED TO DISRESPECT THE THEATER!
THAT MONOLOGUE WAS PURR-FECT!
BUT WE WERE JUST TRYING TO, UH, HELP YOU PROTECT THE SACRED SPACE OF THE THEATER!

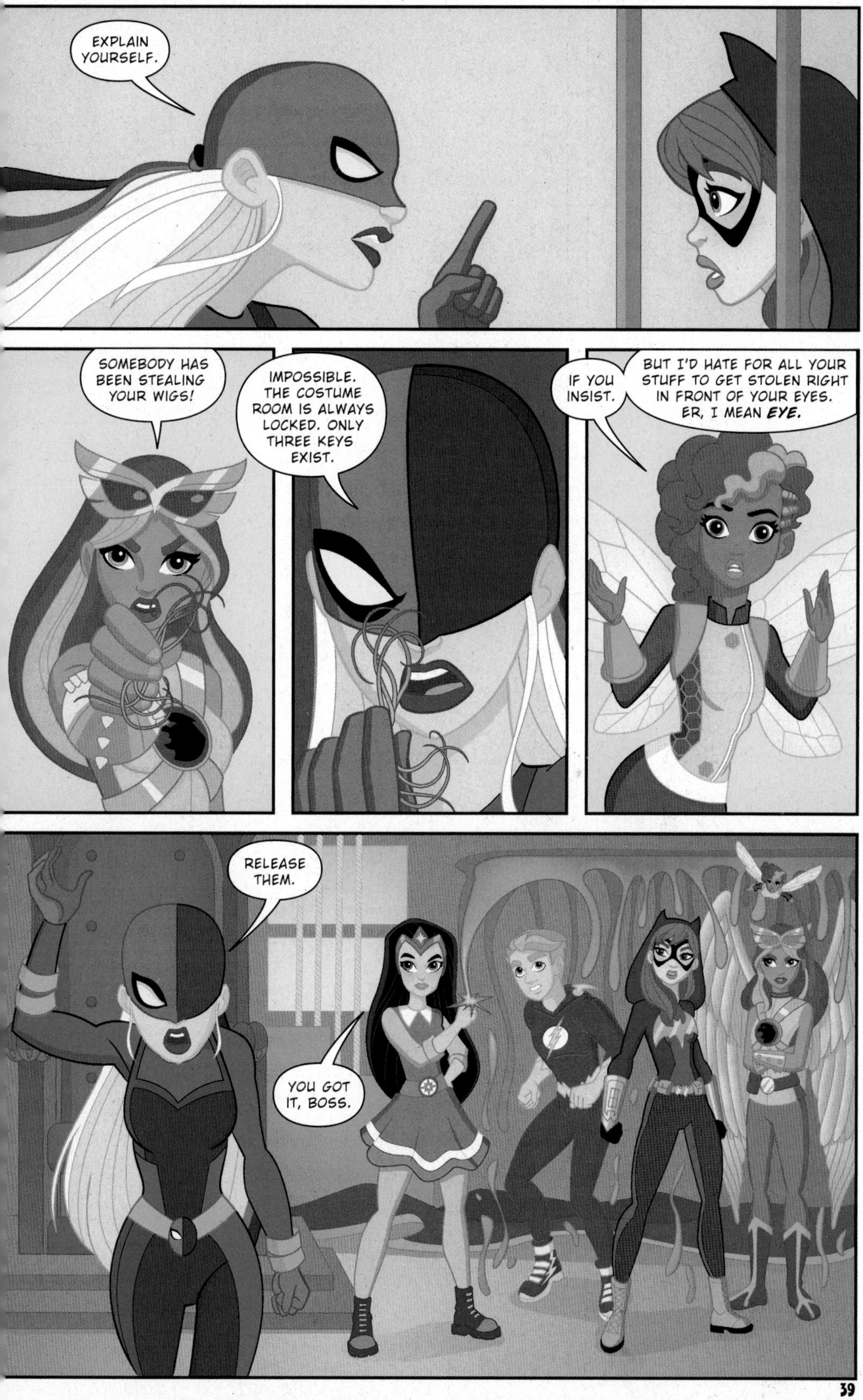

EXPLAIN YOURSELF.
SOMEBODY HAS BEEN STEALING YOUR WIGS!
IMPOSSIBLE. THE COSTUME ROOM IS ALWAYS LOCKED. ONLY THREE KEYS EXIST.
IF YOU INSIST.
BUT I'D HATE FOR ALL YOUR STUFF TO GET STOLEN RIGHT IN FRONT OF YOUR EYES. ER, I MEAN **EYE.**
RELEASE THEM.
YOU GOT IT, BOSS.

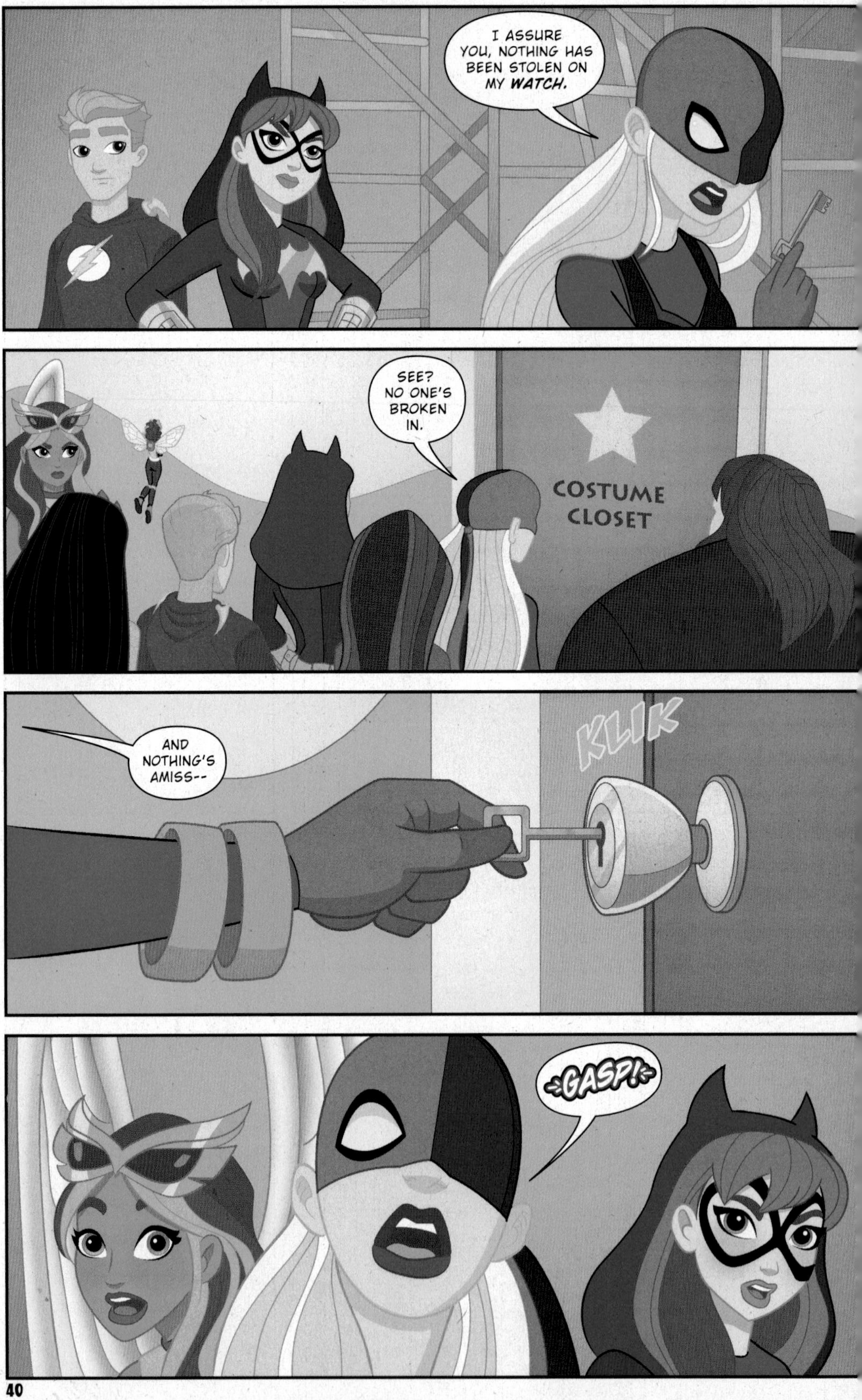
I ASSURE YOU, NOTHING HAS BEEN STOLEN ON MY WATCH.
SEE? NO ONE'S BROKEN IN.
COSTUME CLOSET
AND NOTHING'S AMISS--
KLIK
GASP!

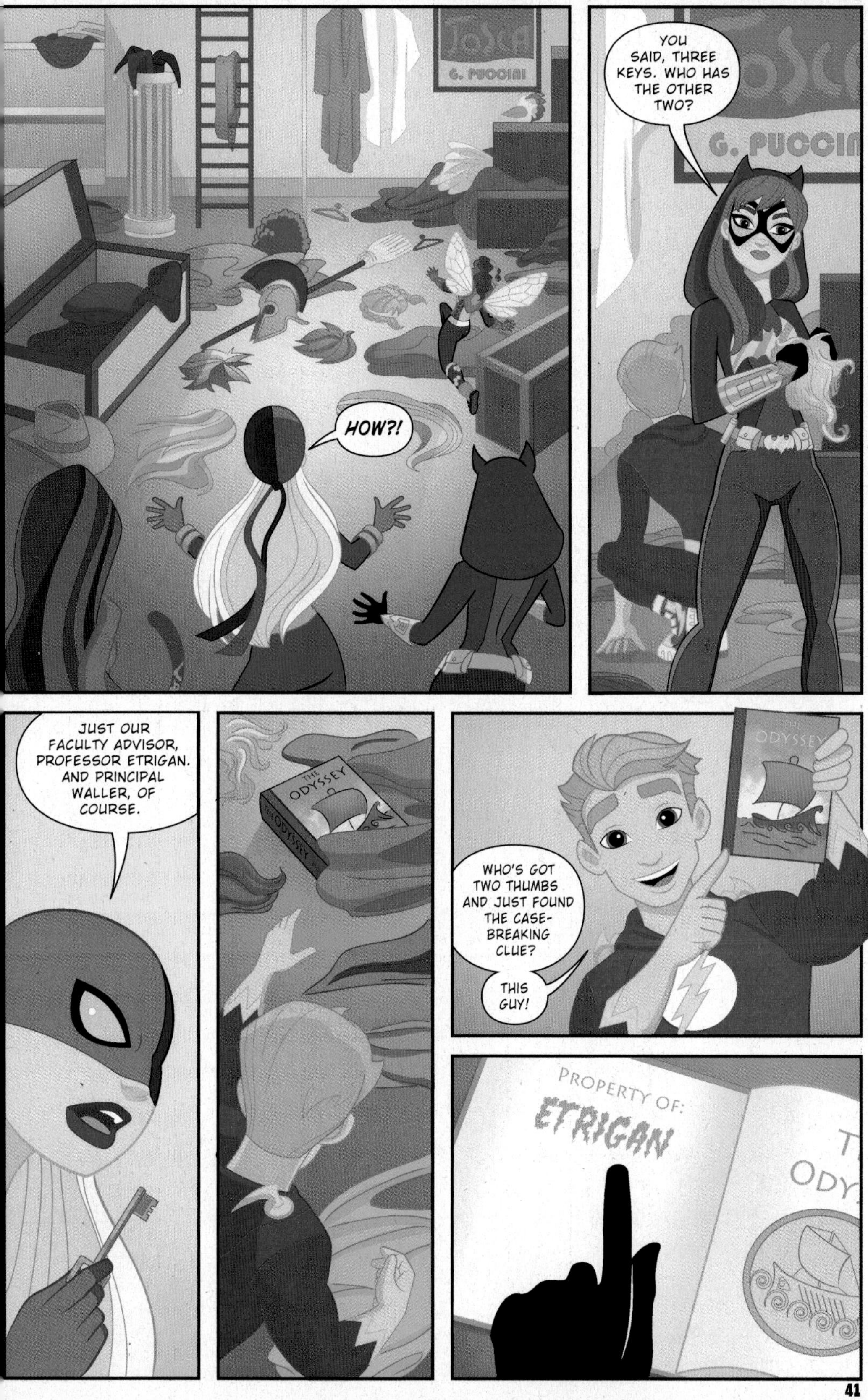
HOW?!
YOU SAID, THREE KEYS. WHO HAS THE OTHER TWO?
JUST OUR FACULTY ADVISOR, PROFESSOR ETRIGAN. AND PRINCIPAL WALLER, OF COURSE.
WHO'S GOT TWO THUMBS AND JUST FOUND THE CASE-BREAKING CLUE?
THIS GUY!
PROPERTY OF:
ETRIGAN

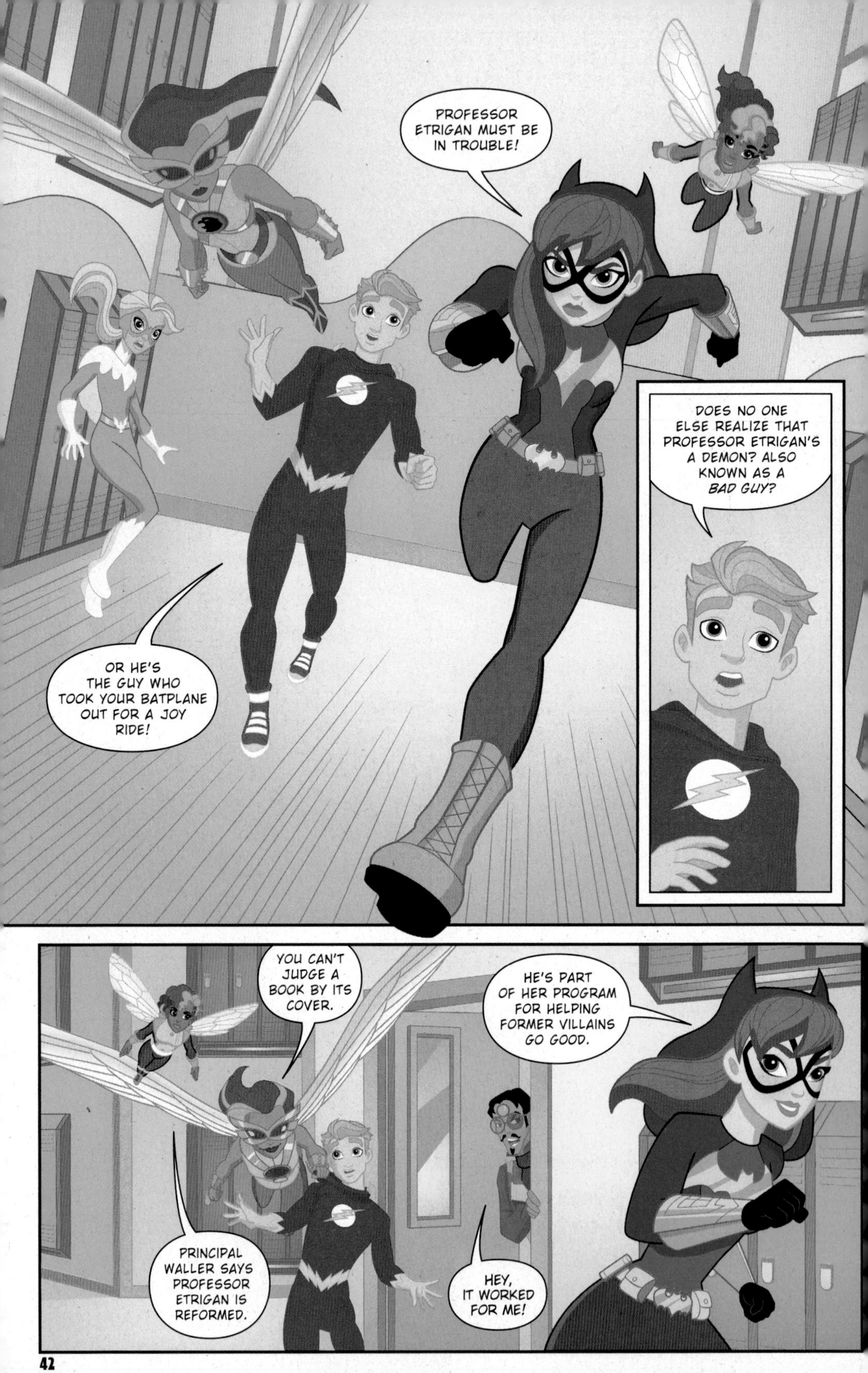
PROFESSOR ETRIGAN MUST BE IN TROUBLE!
OR HE'S THE GUY WHO TOOK YOUR BATPLANE OUT FOR A JOY RIDE!
DOES NO ONE ELSE REALIZE THAT PROFESSOR ETRIGAN'S A DEMON? ALSO KNOWN AS A *BAD GUY*?
PRINCIPAL WALLER SAYS PROFESSOR ETRIGAN IS REFORMED.
YOU CAN'T JUDGE A BOOK BY ITS COVER.
HE'S PART OF HER PROGRAM FOR HELPING FORMER VILLAINS GO GOOD.
HEY, IT WORKED FOR ME!

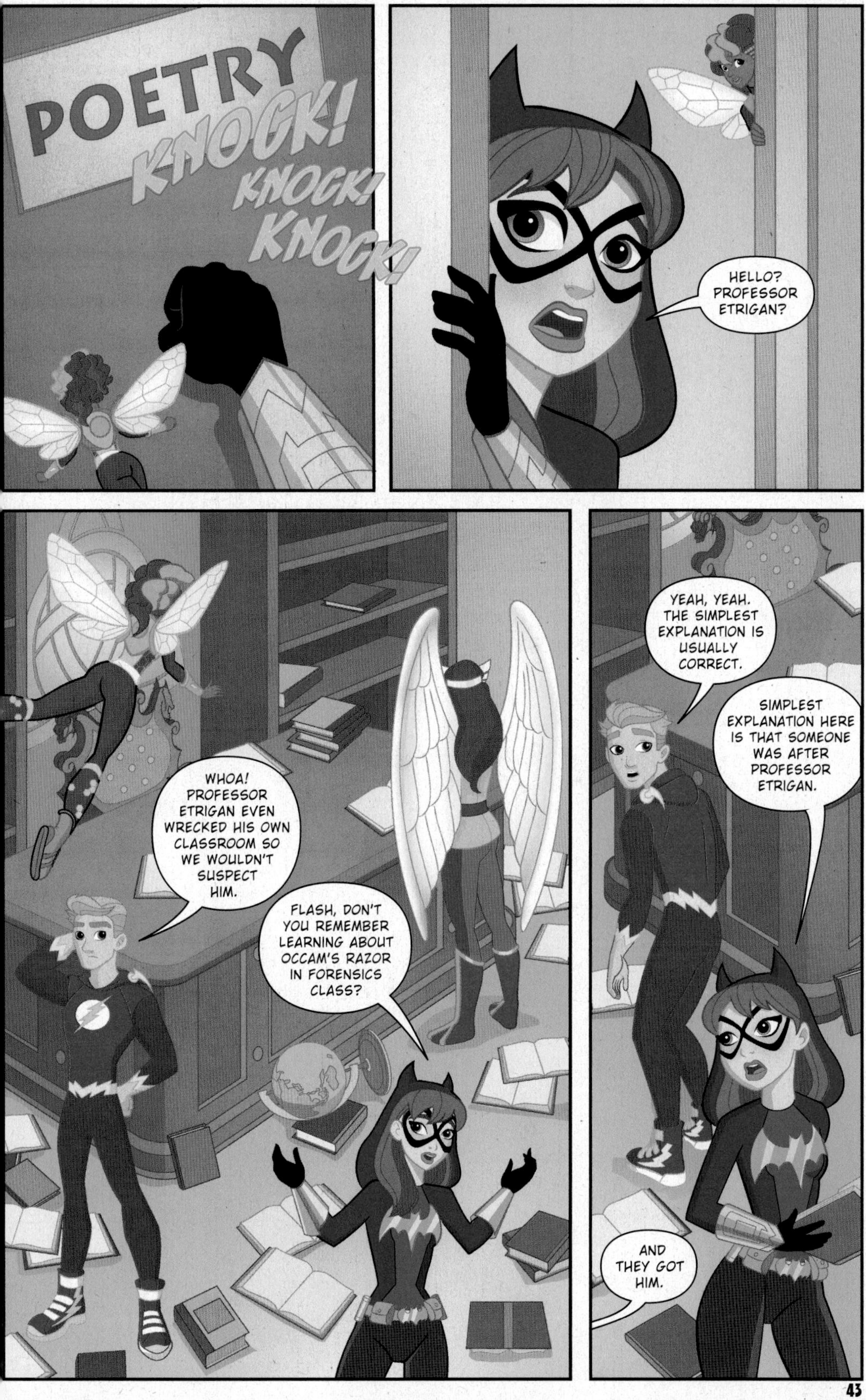
POETRY
KNOCK! KNOCK! KNOCK!
HELLO? PROFESSOR ETRIGAN?
WHOA! PROFESSOR ETRIGAN EVEN WRECKED HIS OWN CLASSROOM SO WE WOULDN'T SUSPECT HIM.
FLASH, DON'T YOU REMEMBER LEARNING ABOUT OCCAM'S RAZOR IN FORENSICS CLASS?
YEAH, YEAH. THE SIMPLEST EXPLANATION IS USUALLY CORRECT.
SIMPLEST EXPLANATION HERE IS THAT SOMEONE WAS AFTER PROFESSOR ETRIGAN.
AND THEY GOT HIM.

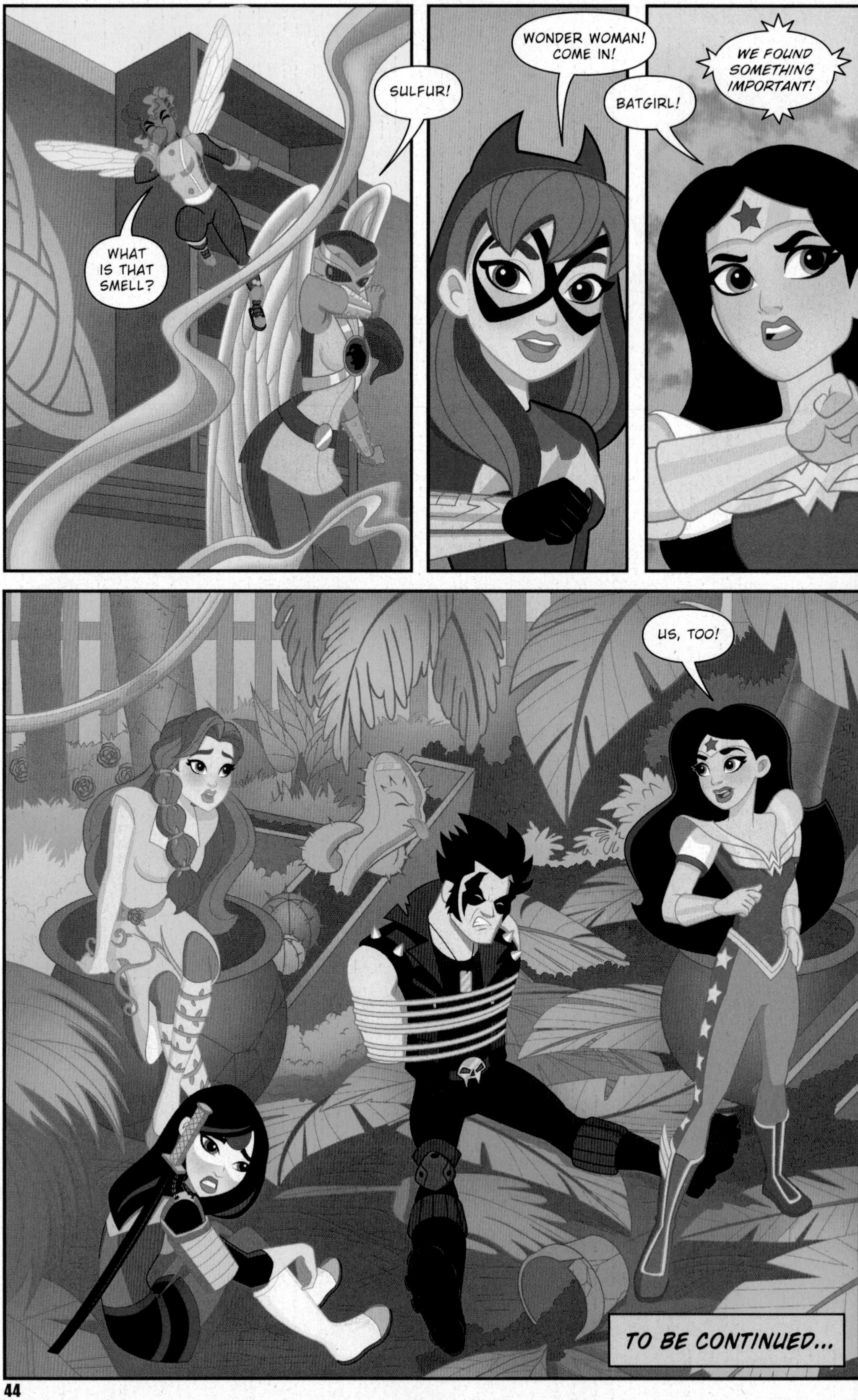
SULFUR!
WHAT IS THAT SMELL?
WONDER WOMAN! COME IN!
BATGIRL!
WE FOUND SOMETHING IMPORTANT!
US, TOO!
TO BE CONTINUED...

CHAPTER THREE
THE WITCH

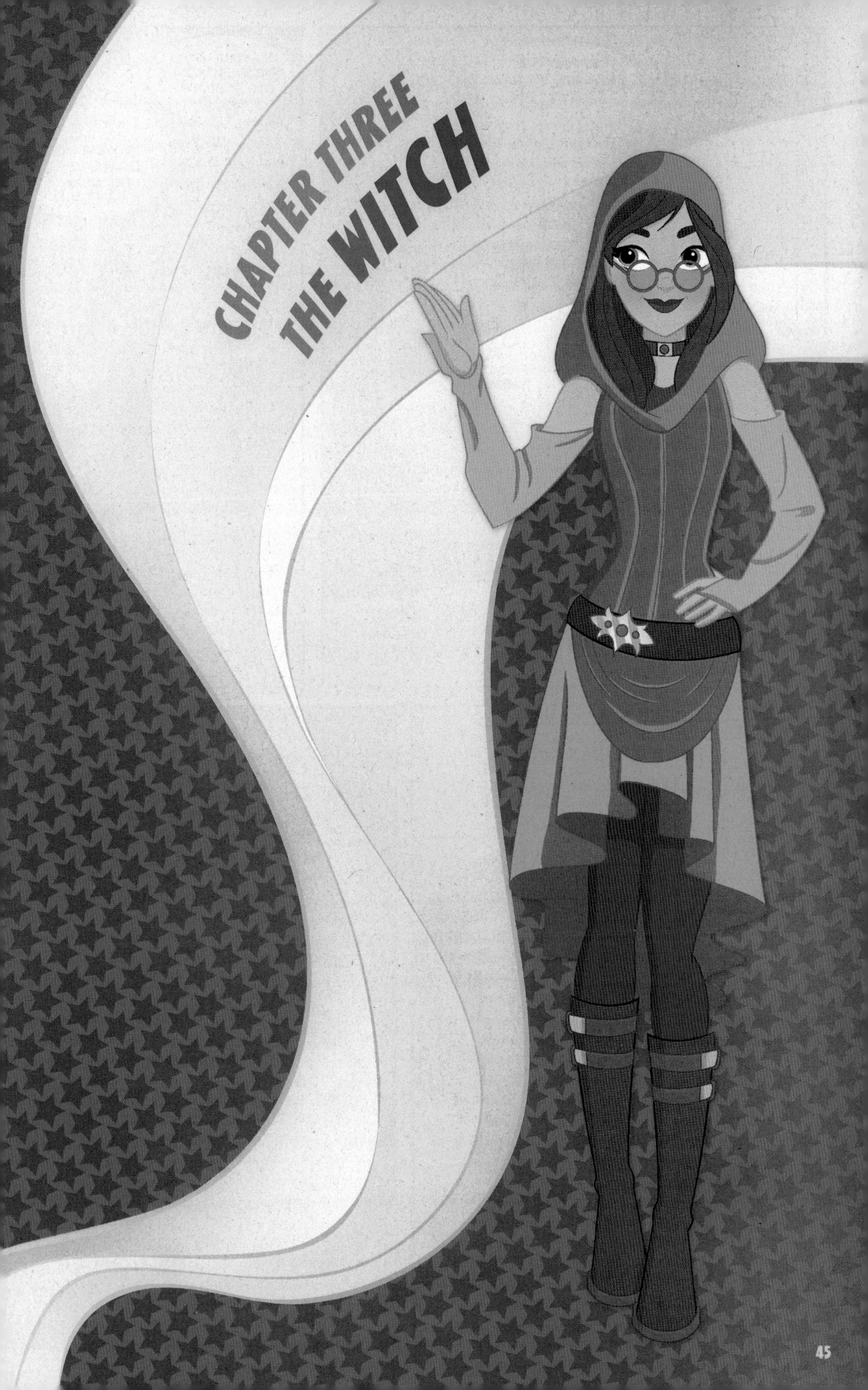

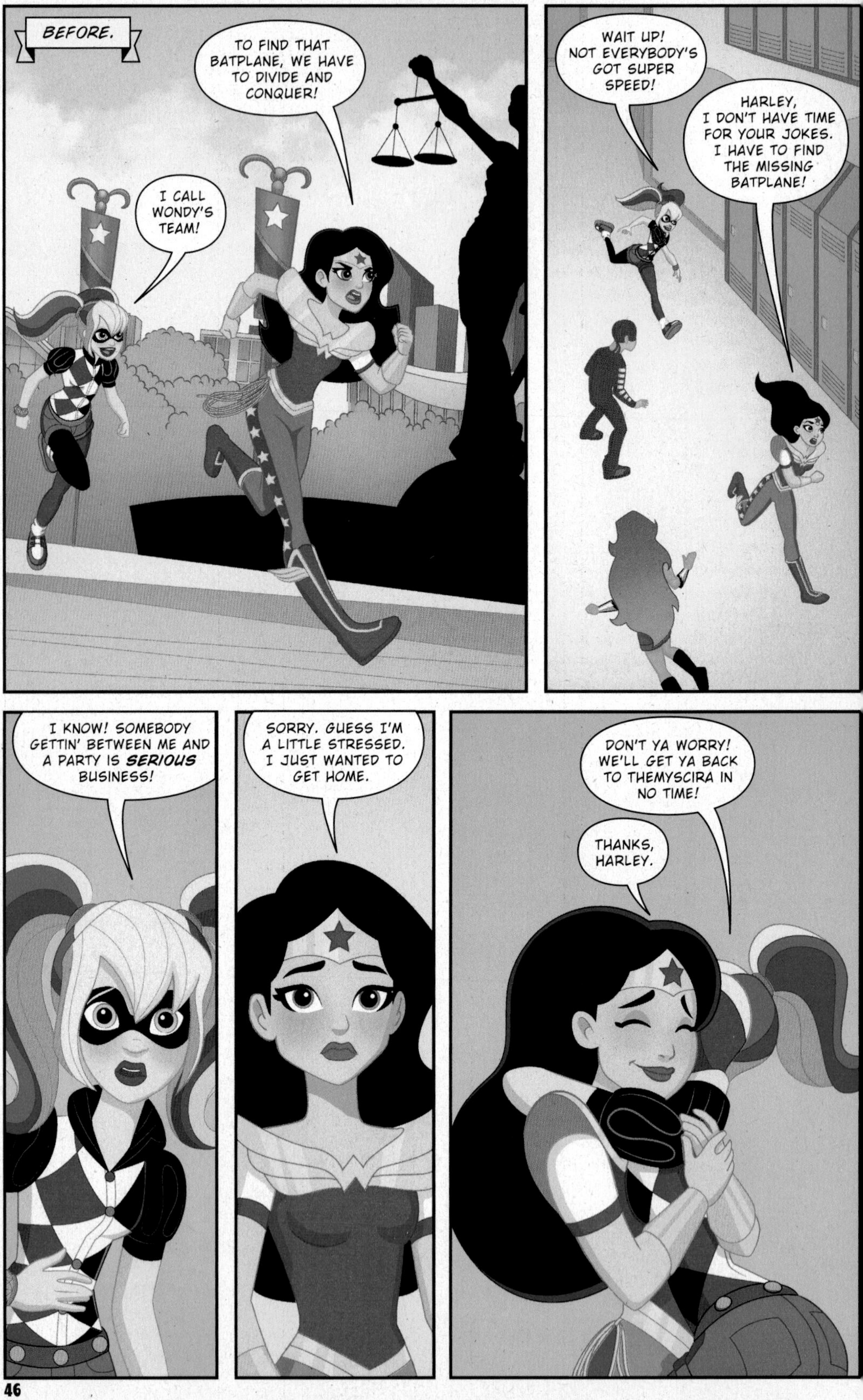
BEFORE.
TO FIND THAT BATPLANE, WE HAVE TO DIVIDE AND CONQUER!
I CALL WONDY'S TEAM!
WAIT UP! NOT EVERYBODY'S GOT SUPER SPEED!
HARLEY, I DON'T HAVE TIME FOR YOUR JOKES. I HAVE TO FIND THE MISSING BATPLANE!
I KNOW! SOMEBODY GETTIN' BETWEEN ME AND A PARTY IS SERIOUS BUSINESS!
SORRY. GUESS I'M A LITTLE STRESSED. I JUST WANTED TO GET HOME.
DON'T YA WORRY! WE'LL GET YA BACK TO THEMYSCIRA IN NO TIME!
THANKS, HARLEY.

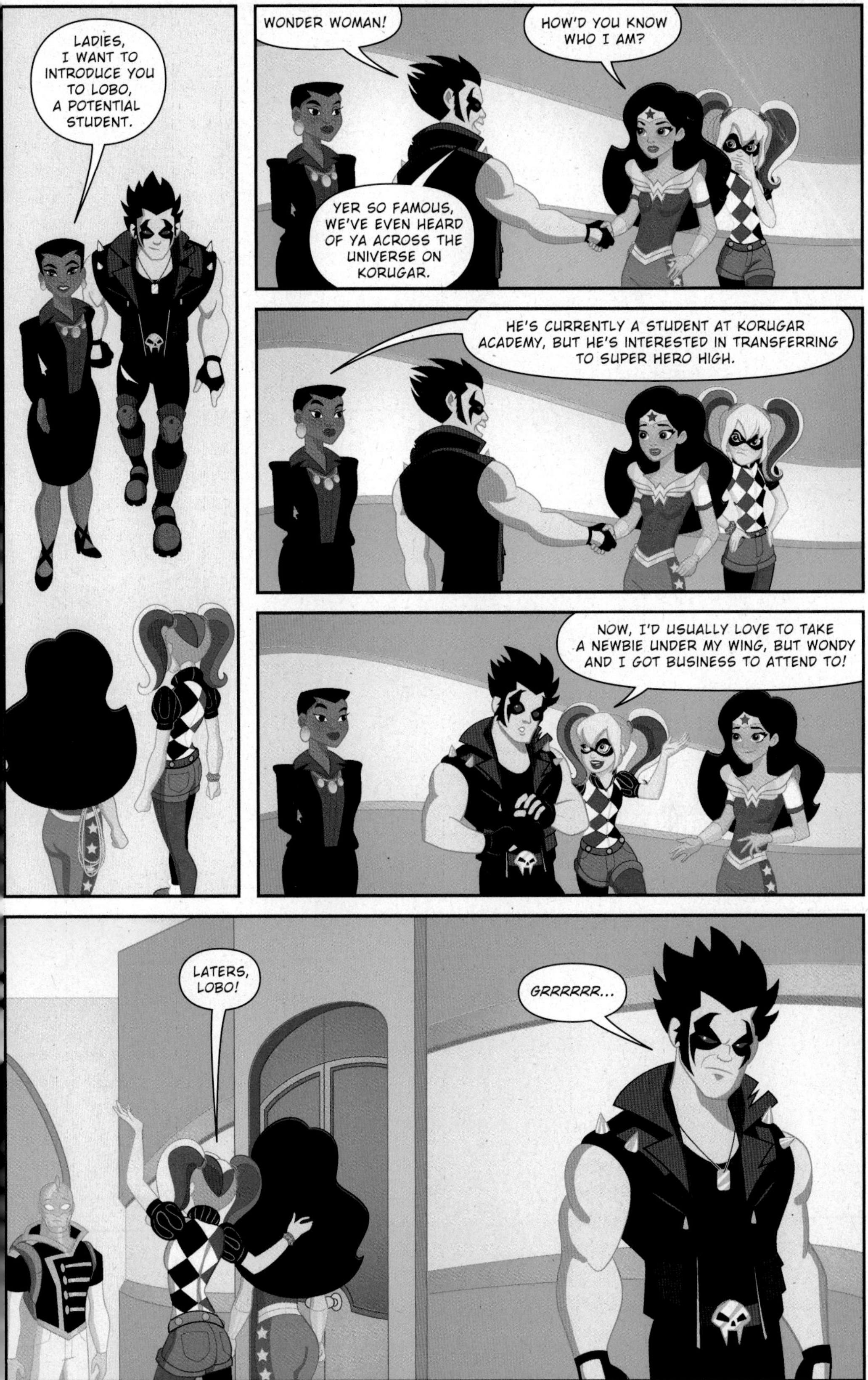
LADIES, I WANT TO INTRODUCE YOU TO LOBO, A POTENTIAL STUDENT.
WONDER WOMAN!
HOW'D YOU KNOW WHO I AM?
YER SO FAMOUS, WE'VE EVEN HEARD OF YA ACROSS THE UNIVERSE ON KORUGAR.
HE'S CURRENTLY A STUDENT AT KORUGAR ACADEMY, BUT HE'S INTERESTED IN TRANSFERRING TO SUPER HERO HIGH.
NOW, I'D USUALLY LOVE TO TAKE A NEWBIE UNDER MY WING, BUT WONDY AND I GOT BUSINESS TO ATTEND TO!
LATERS, LOBO!
GRRRRRR...

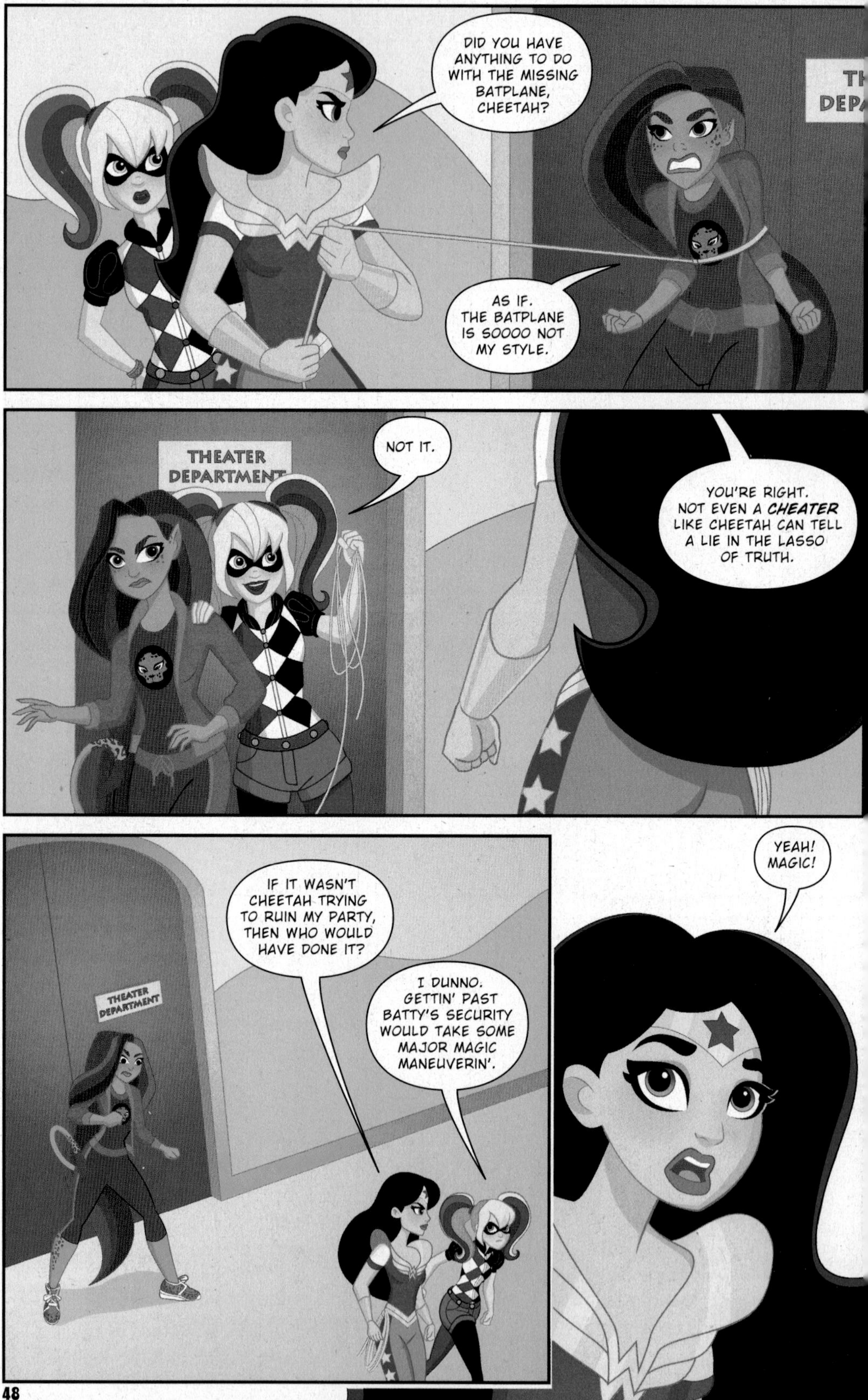

DID YOU HAVE ANYTHING TO DO WITH THE MISSING BATPLANE, CHEETAH?
AS IF. THE BATPLANE IS SOOOO NOT MY STYLE.
THEATER DEPARTMENT
NOT IT.
YOU'RE RIGHT. NOT EVEN A **CHEATER** LIKE CHEETAH CAN TELL A LIE IN THE LASSO OF TRUTH.
IF IT WASN'T CHEETAH TRYING TO RUIN MY PARTY, THEN WHO WOULD HAVE DONE IT?
THEATER DEPARTMENT
I DUNNO. GETTIN' PAST BATTY'S SECURITY WOULD TAKE SOME MAJOR MAGIC MANEUVERIN'.
YEAH! MAGIC!

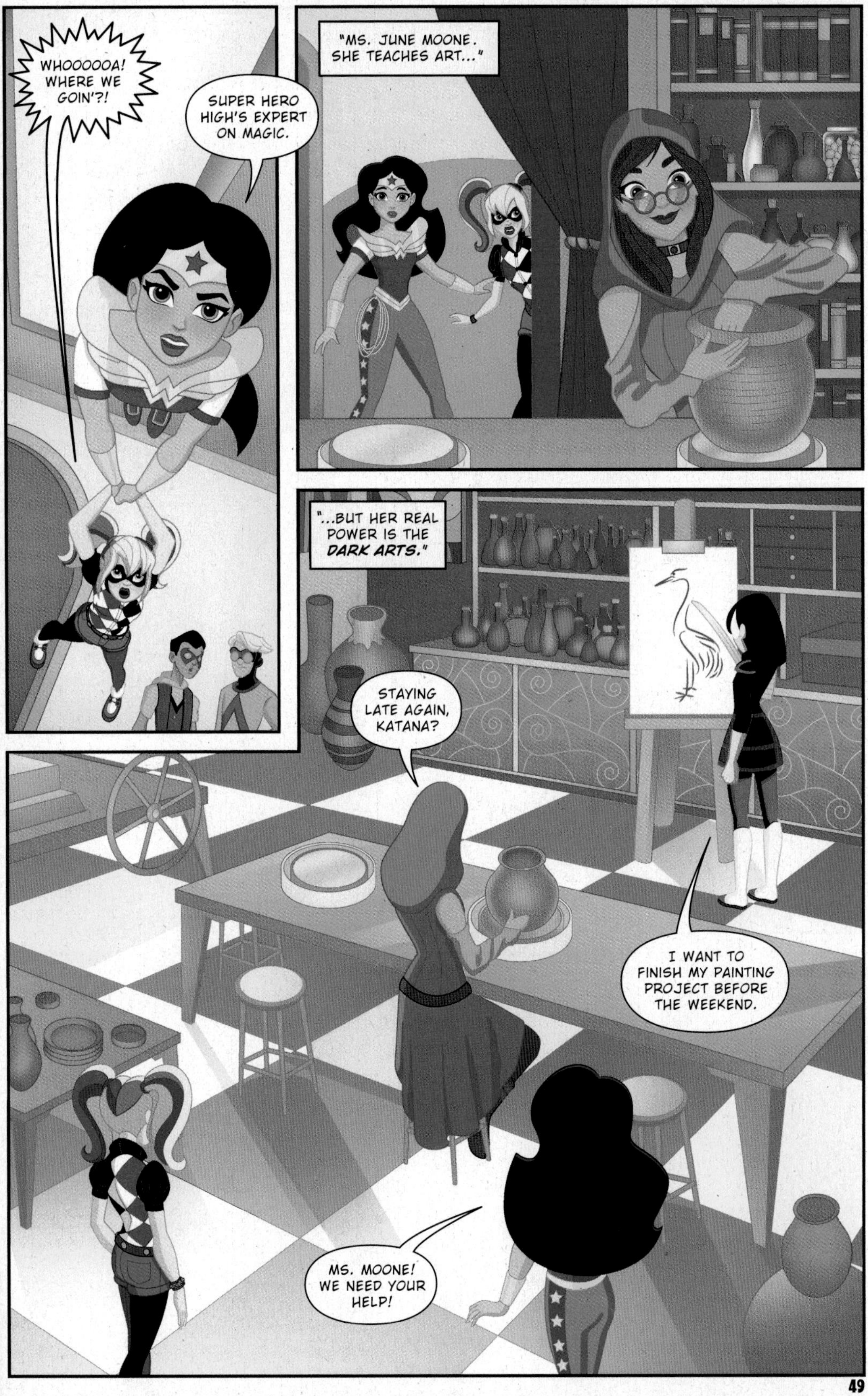

WHOOOOOA! WHERE WE GOIN'?!
SUPER HERO HIGH'S EXPERT ON MAGIC.
"MS. JUNE MOONE. SHE TEACHES ART..."
"...BUT HER REAL POWER IS THE *DARK ARTS.*"
STAYING LATE AGAIN, KATANA?
I WANT TO FINISH MY PAINTING PROJECT BEFORE THE WEEKEND.
MS. MOONE! WE NEED YOUR HELP!

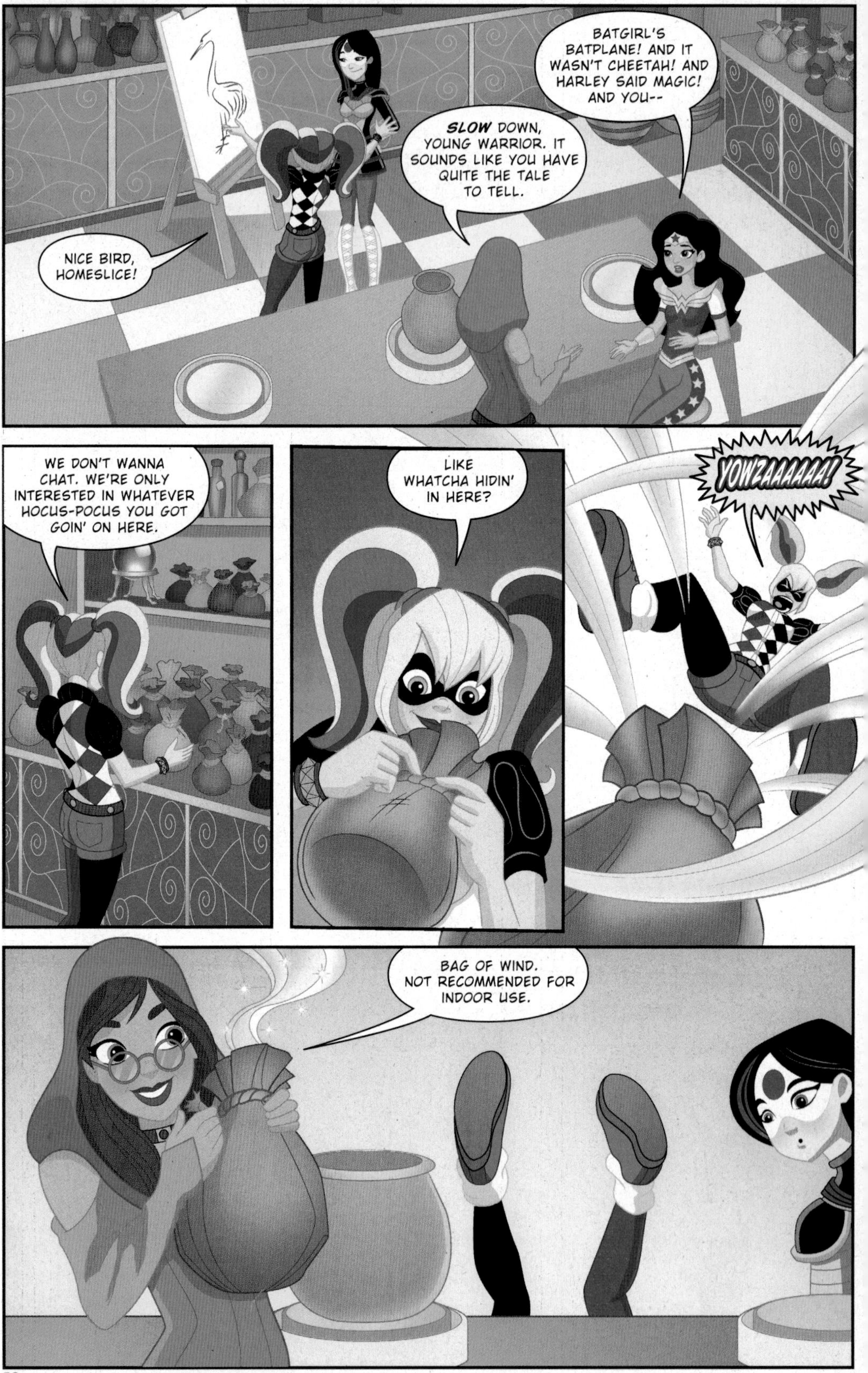
BATGIRL'S BATPLANE! AND IT WASN'T CHEETAH! AND HARLEY SAID MAGIC! AND YOU--
SLOW DOWN, YOUNG WARRIOR. IT SOUNDS LIKE YOU HAVE QUITE THE TALE TO TELL.
NICE BIRD, HOMESLICE!
WE DON'T WANNA CHAT. WE'RE ONLY INTERESTED IN WHATEVER HOCUS-POCUS YOU GOT GOIN' ON HERE.
LIKE WHATCHA HIDIN' IN HERE?
YOWZAAAAAA!
BAG OF WIND. NOT RECOMMENDED FOR INDOOR USE.

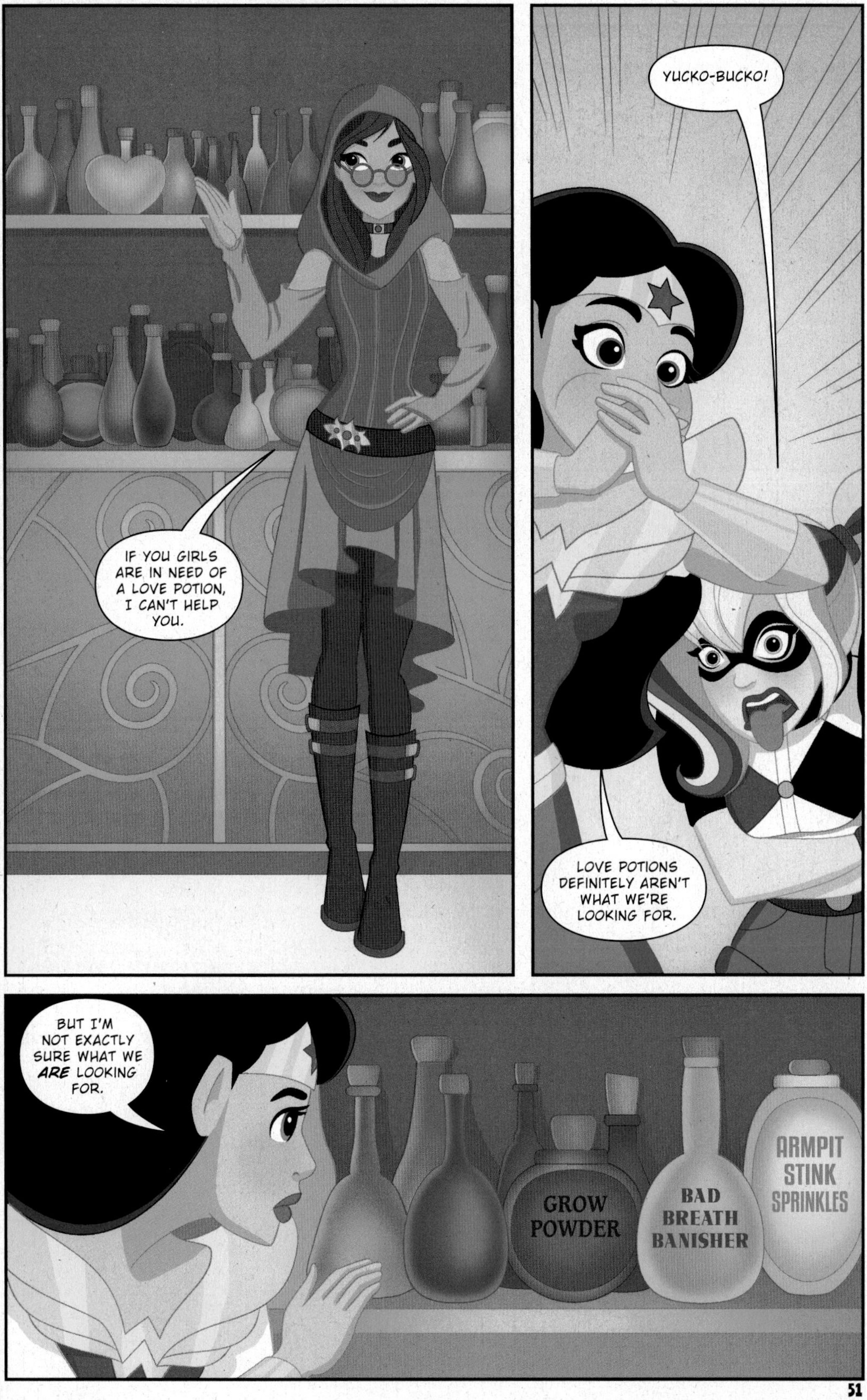
IF YOU GIRLS ARE IN NEED OF A LOVE POTION, I CAN'T HELP YOU.
YUCKO-BUCKO!
LOVE POTIONS DEFINITELY AREN'T WHAT WE'RE LOOKING FOR.
BUT I'M NOT EXACTLY SURE WHAT WE *ARE* LOOKING FOR.
GROW POWDER
BAD BREATH BANISHER
ARMPIT STINK SPRINKLES

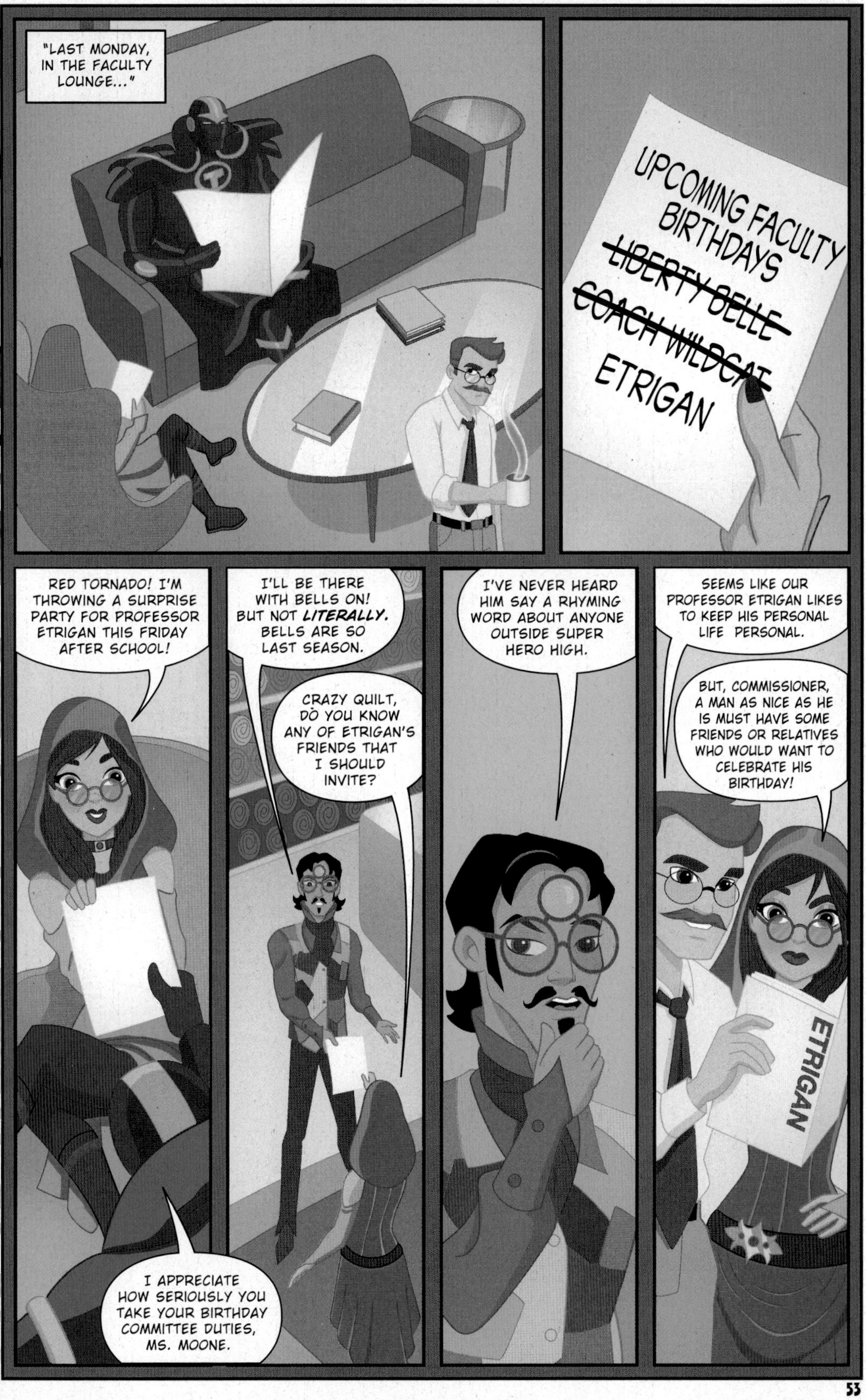
"LAST MONDAY, IN THE FACULTY LOUNGE..."
UPCOMING FACULTY BIRTHDAYS
LIBERTY BELLE
COACH WILDCAT
ETRIGAN
RED TORNADO! I'M THROWING A SURPRISE PARTY FOR PROFESSOR ETRIGAN THIS FRIDAY AFTER SCHOOL!
I APPRECIATE HOW SERIOUSLY YOU TAKE YOUR BIRTHDAY COMMITTEE DUTIES, MS. MOONE.
I'LL BE THERE WITH BELLS ON! BUT NOT ***LITERALLY.*** BELLS ARE SO LAST SEASON.
CRAZY QUILT, DO YOU KNOW ANY OF ETRIGAN'S FRIENDS THAT I SHOULD INVITE?
I'VE NEVER HEARD HIM SAY A RHYMING WORD ABOUT ANYONE OUTSIDE SUPER HERO HIGH.
SEEMS LIKE OUR PROFESSOR ETRIGAN LIKES TO KEEP HIS PERSONAL LIFE PERSONAL.
BUT, COMMISSIONER, A MAN AS NICE AS HE IS MUST HAVE SOME FRIENDS OR RELATIVES WHO WOULD WANT TO CELEBRATE HIS BIRTHDAY!
ETRIGAN

"AND THEN, TODAY, AFTER SCHOOL..."

ALL RIGHT, TEAM. ON THREE, WE GIVE IT OUR ALL. ONE. TWO.

TO: ALL CONTACTS
SUBJECT: CELEBRATE PROFESSOR ETRIGAN!

Send

PLEASE, COACH WILDCAT, WE KNOW HOW TO SURPRISE.

SURPRISE!

HAPPY BIRTHDAY! SORRY I COULDN'T GET THE INVITE TO ANY OF YOUR NON-SCHOOL FRIENDS.

MY FRIENDS?!

I SENT EMAILS ACROSS THE GALAXY! BUT NOT A SINGLE R.S.V.P.!

PROFESSOR ETRIGAN? WHAT'S WRONG? DO YOU PREFER CHOCOLATE CAKE?

"I GAVE PROFESSOR ERTIGAN THE ULTIMATE UNLOCKER AS HIS BIRTHDAY GIFT..."

"BUT HE RAN AWAY WITHOUT EVEN THANKING ME FOR THE POTION..."

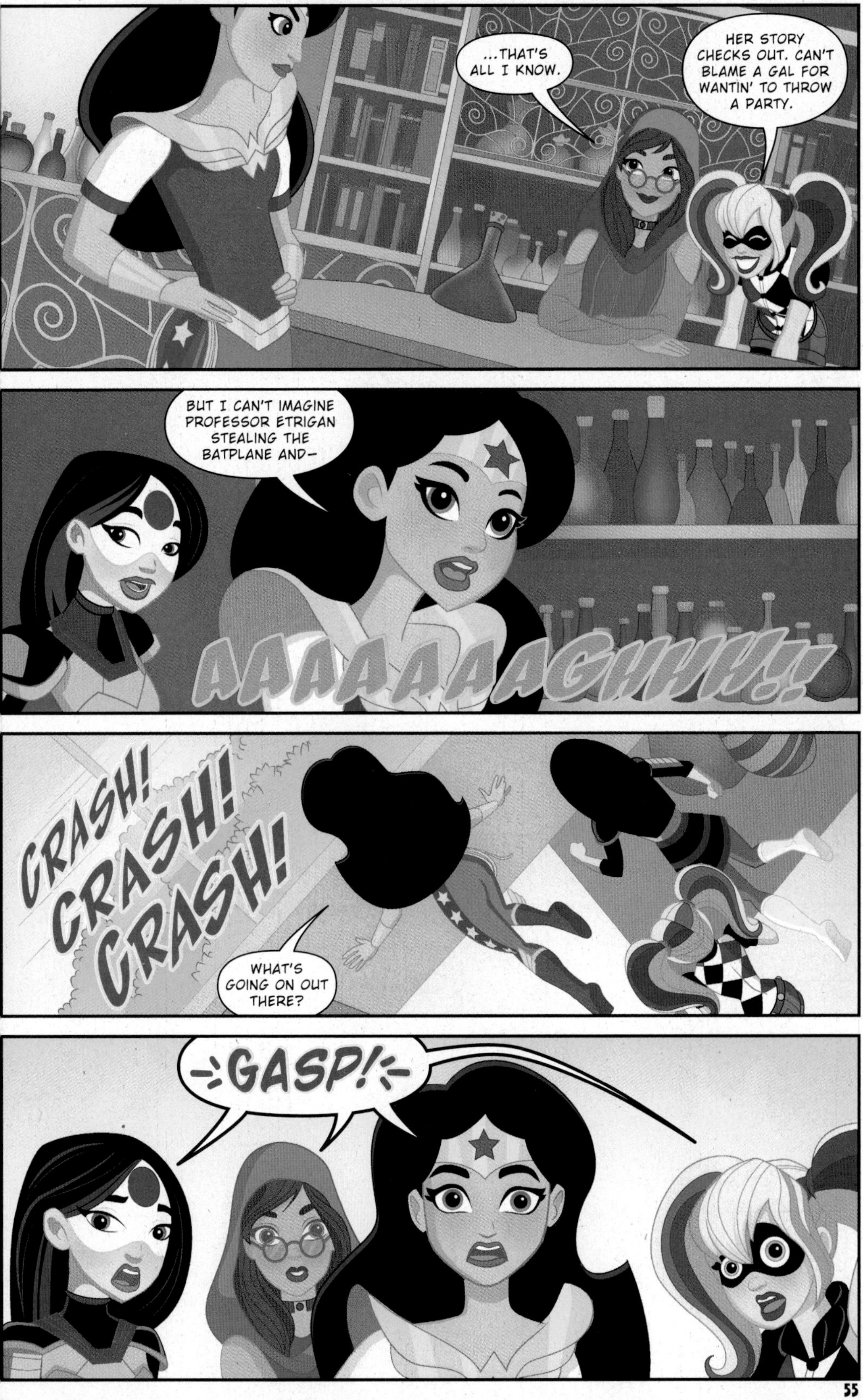
...THAT'S ALL I KNOW.
HER STORY CHECKS OUT. CAN'T BLAME A GAL FOR WANTIN' TO THROW A PARTY.
BUT I CAN'T IMAGINE PROFESSOR ETRIGAN STEALING THE BATPLANE AND—
AAAAAAAAGHHH!!
CRASH! CRASH! CRASH!
WHAT'S GOING ON OUT THERE?
GASP!

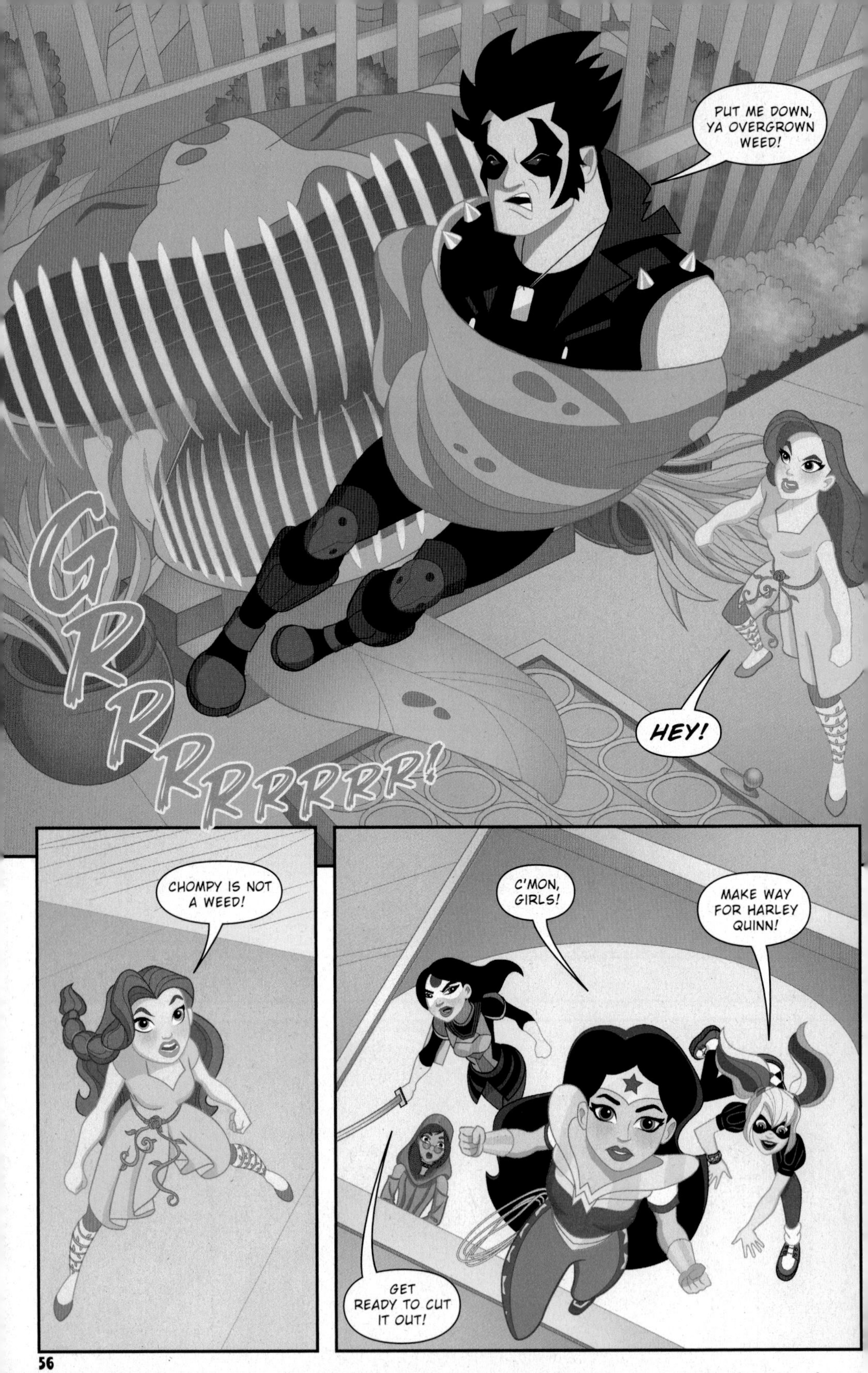
PUT ME DOWN, YA OVERGROWN WEED!
GRRRRRRRRR!
HEY!
CHOMPY IS NOT A WEED!
C'MON, GIRLS!
MAKE WAY FOR HARLEY QUINN!
GET READY TO CUT IT OUT!

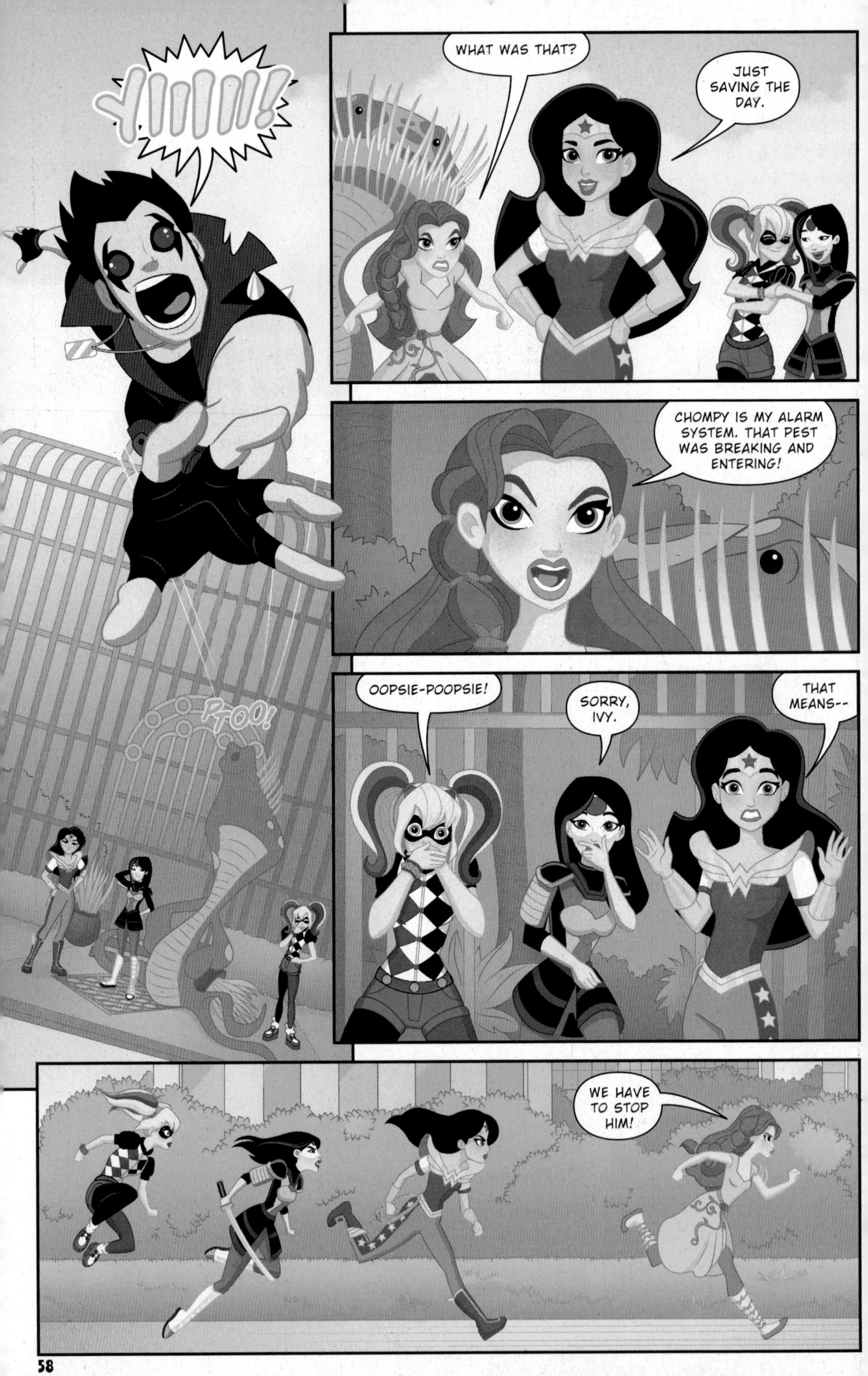
YIIIII!
PTOO!
WHAT WAS THAT?
JUST SAVING THE DAY.
CHOMPY IS MY ALARM SYSTEM. THAT PEST WAS BREAKING AND ENTERING!
OOPSIE-POOPSIE!
SORRY, IVY.
THAT MEANS--
WE HAVE TO STOP HIM!

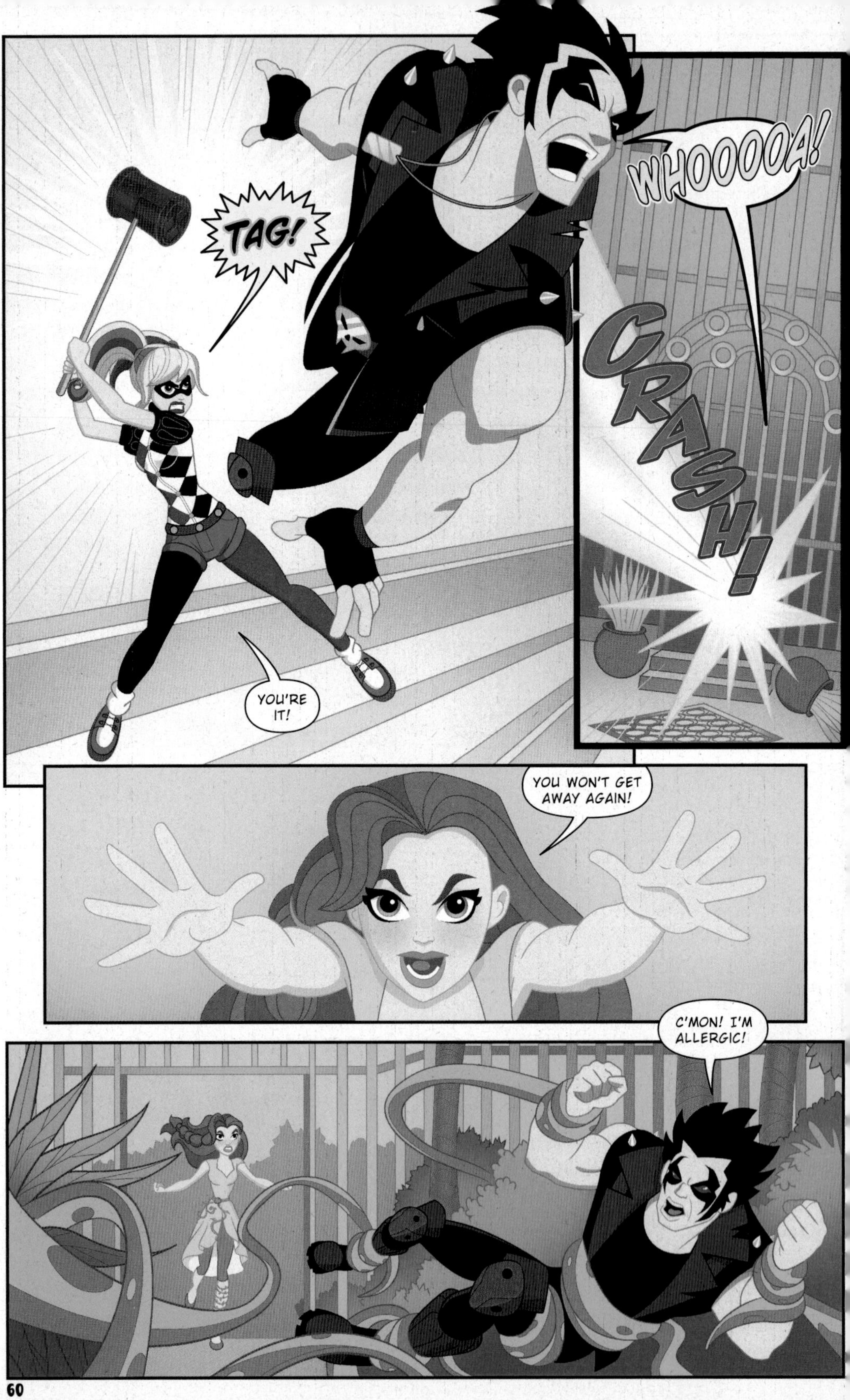
TAG!
WHOOOOOA!
CRASH!
YOU'RE IT!
YOU WON'T GET AWAY AGAIN!
C'MON! I'M ALLERGIC!

62

CHAPTER FOUR
THE SIRENS

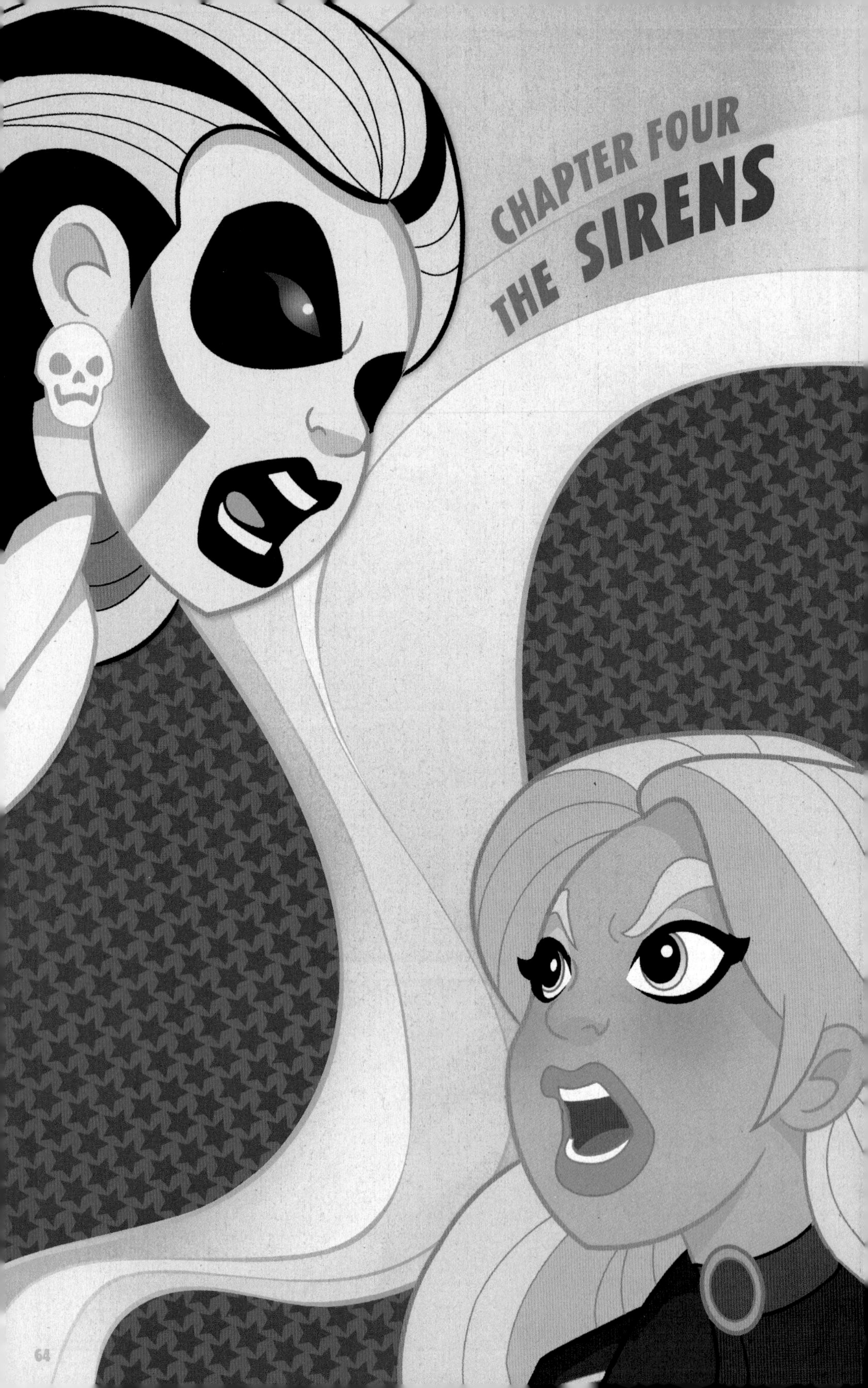

67

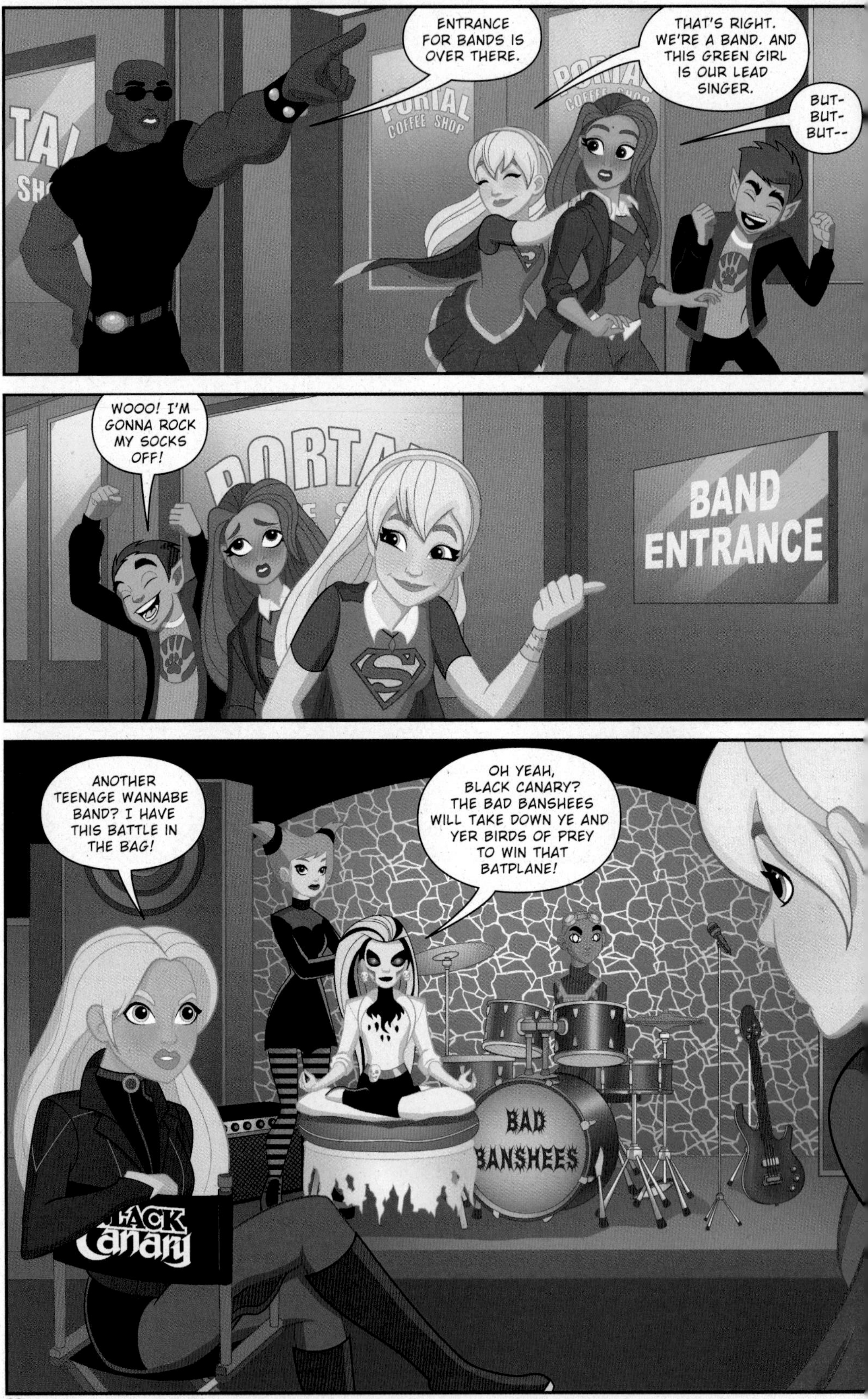

ENTRANCE FOR BANDS IS OVER THERE.
THAT'S RIGHT. WE'RE A BAND. AND THIS GREEN GIRL IS OUR LEAD SINGER.
BUT-BUT-BUT--
PORTAL COFFEE SHOP
WOOO! I'M GONNA ROCK MY SOCKS OFF!
BAND ENTRANCE
ANOTHER TEENAGE WANNABE BAND? I HAVE THIS BATTLE IN THE BAG!
OH YEAH, BLACK CANARY? THE BAD BANSHEES WILL TAKE DOWN YE AND YER BIRDS OF PREY TO WIN THAT BATPLANE!
BAD BANSHEES

SILVER BANSHEE! HOW'D YOU DO ON YOUR HERO HISTORY TEST?

NO TIME FOR CHATTIN'. I GOTTA BATPLANE TO WIN!

HOW DOES A COFFEE SHOP GET ONE OF THOSE? HMMMM?

THE RULES-- LIKE EVERYTHIN' ELSE AT THE PORTAL--ARE STRANGE.

"IT'S *FINDERS KEEPERS*. LOSE IT HERE AND IT GOES IN THE PRIZE BIN. TODAY, SOMEBODY LOST THE BATPLANE."

AND WE'RE GOING TO FIND IT!

YOU DON'T NEED SUPER SMELLING TO SMELL THAT!

THAT'S WORSE THAN THE BOY'S DORM AFTER TACO TUESDAY!

SULFUR?!

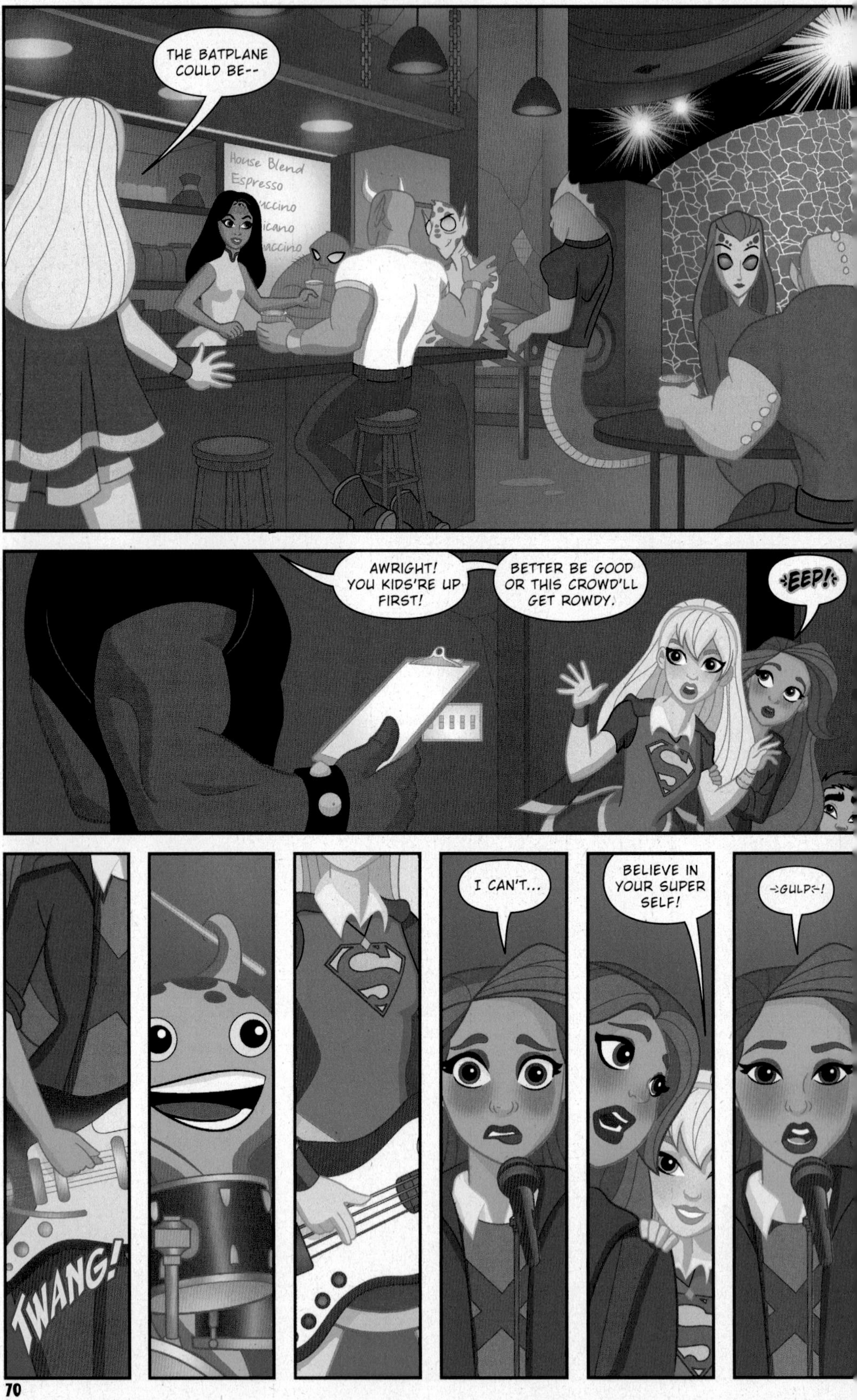
THE BATPLANE COULD BE--
House Blend
Espresso
AWRIGHT! YOU KIDS'RE UP FIRST!
BETTER BE GOOD OR THIS CROWD'LL GET ROWDY.
EEP!
TWANG!
I CAN'T...
BELIEVE IN YOUR SUPER SELF!
GULP!

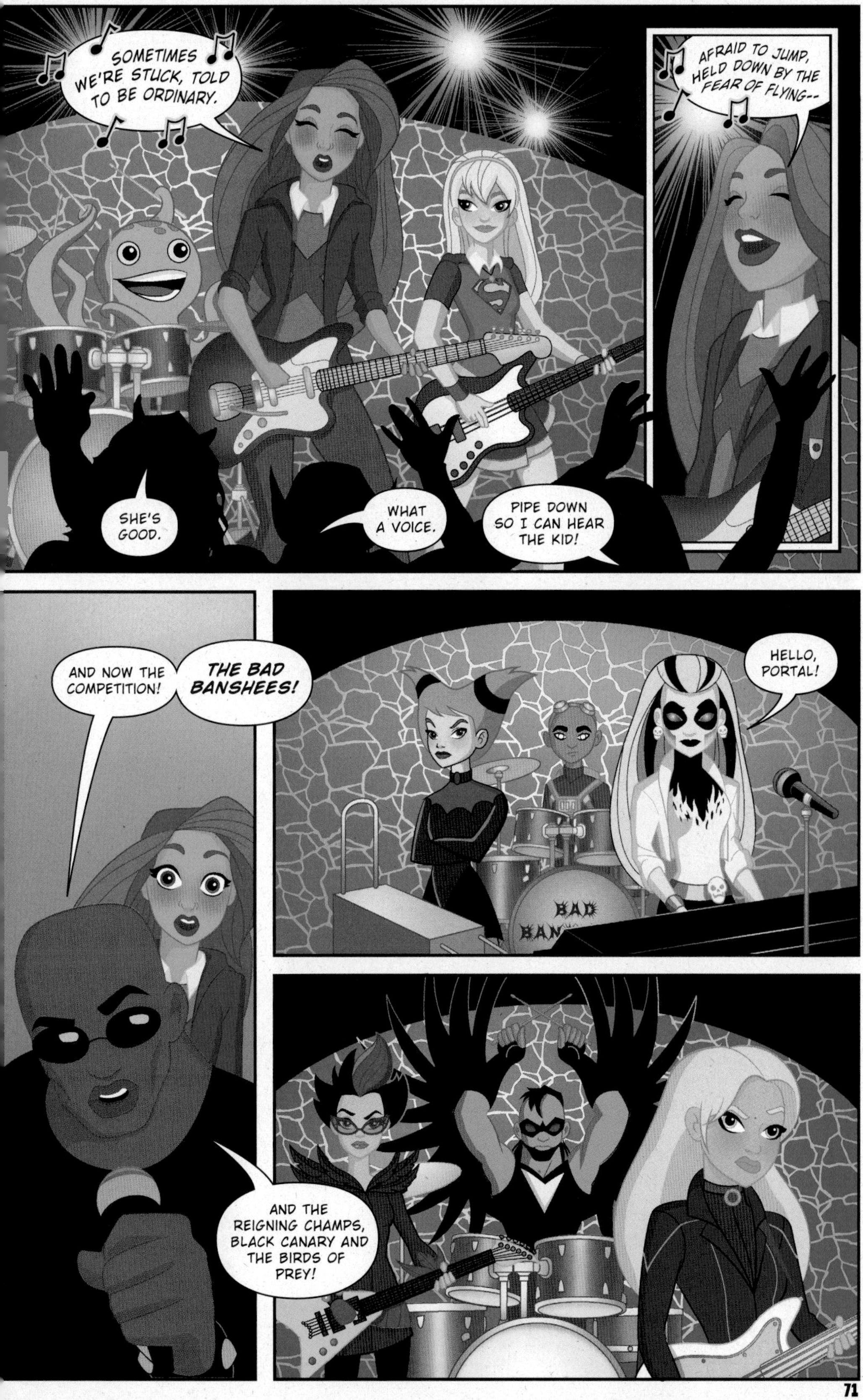
SOMETIMES WE'RE STUCK, TOLD TO BE ORDINARY.
AFRAID TO JUMP, HELD DOWN BY THE FEAR OF FLYING--
SHE'S GOOD.
WHAT A VOICE.
PIPE DOWN SO I CAN HEAR THE KID!
AND NOW THE COMPETITION!
THE BAD BANSHEES!
HELLO, PORTAL!
AND THE REIGNING CHAMPS, BLACK CANARY AND THE BIRDS OF PREY!

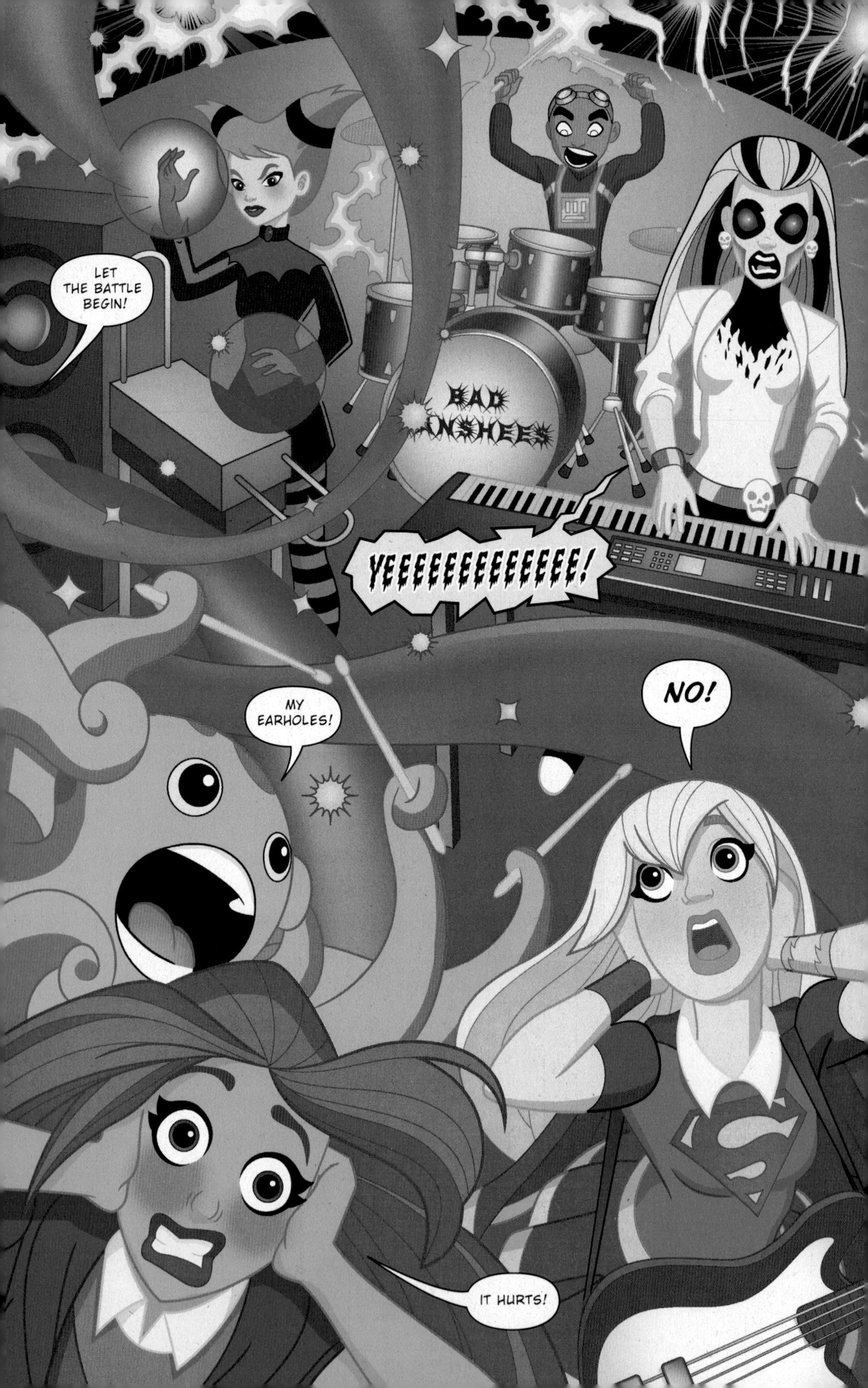
LET THE BATTLE BEGIN!
BAD ANSHEES
YEEEEEEEEEEEEE!
MY EARHOLES!
NO!
IT HURTS!

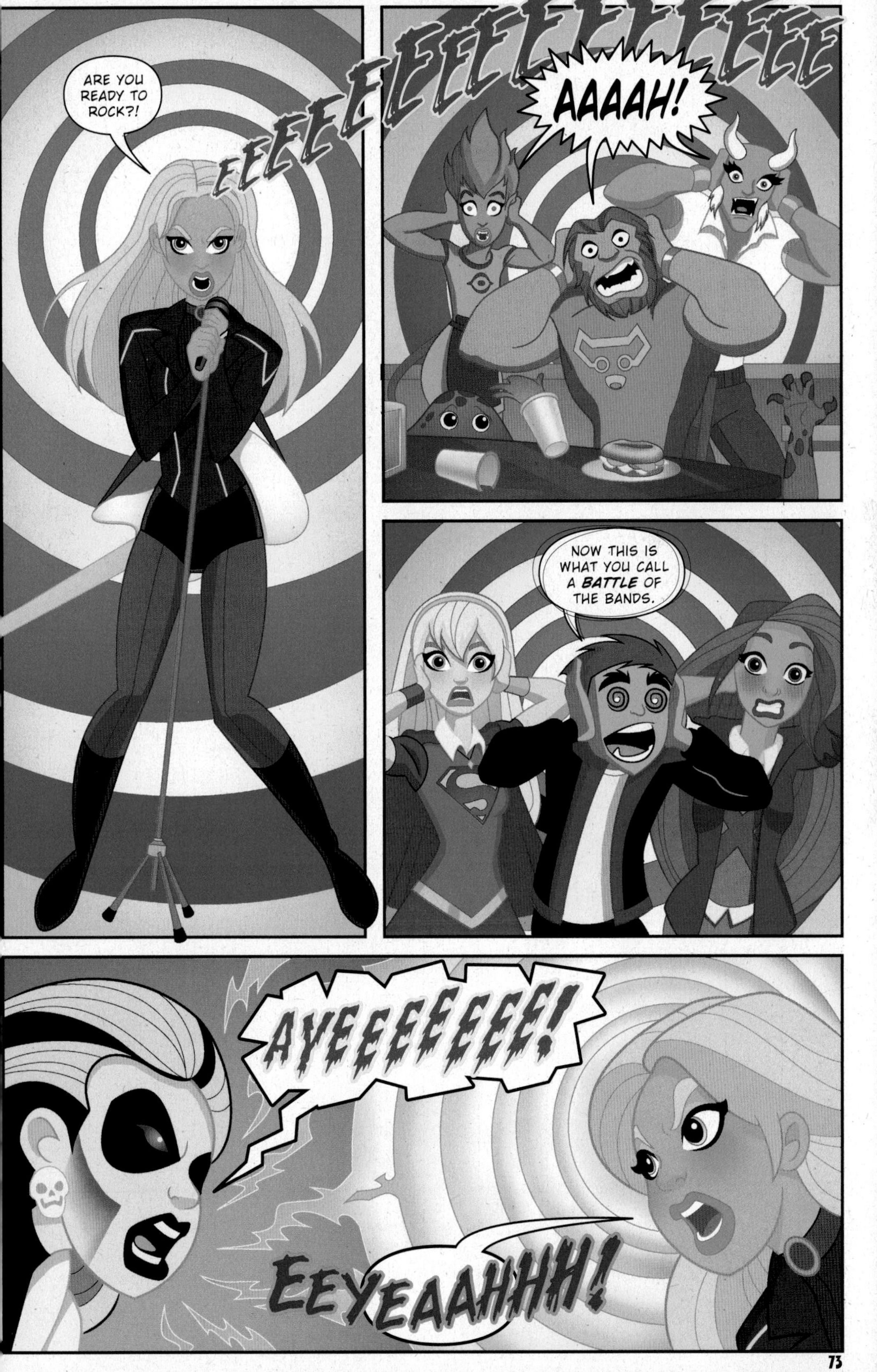
ARE YOU READY TO ROCK?!
EEEEEEEEEEEEEEEEEE
AAAAH!
NOW THIS IS WHAT YOU CALL A *BATTLE* OF THE BANDS.
AYEEEEEEEE!
EEYEAAHHH!

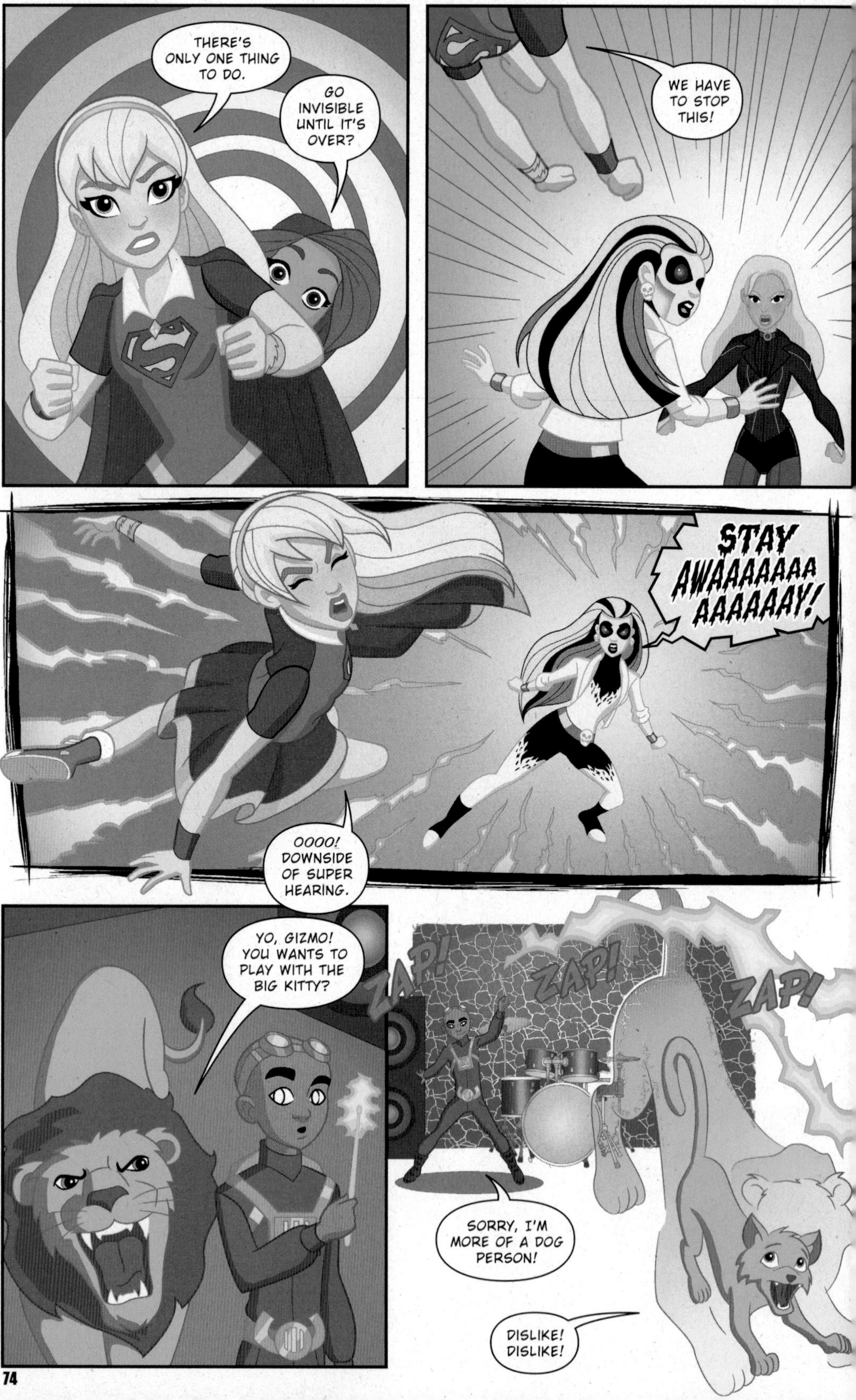
THERE'S ONLY ONE THING TO DO.
GO INVISIBLE UNTIL IT'S OVER?
WE HAVE TO STOP THIS!
STAY AWAAAAAAAAAAAAAAY!
OOOO! DOWNSIDE OF SUPER HEARING.
YO, GIZMO! YOU WANTS TO PLAY WITH THE BIG KITTY?
ZAP!
ZAP!
ZAP!
SORRY, I'M MORE OF A DOG PERSON!
DISLIKE! DISLIKE!

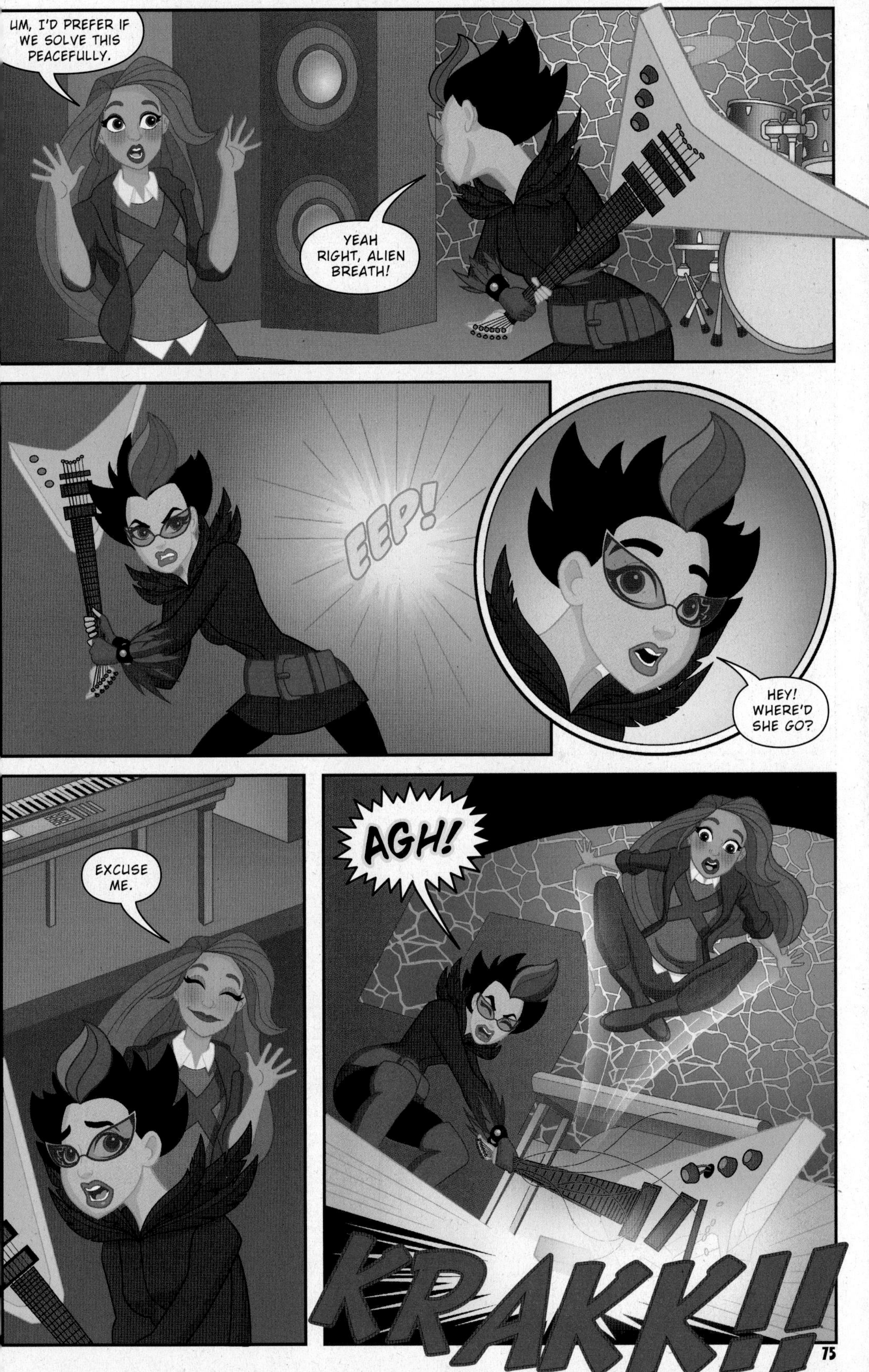
UM, I'D PREFER IF WE SOLVE THIS PEACEFULLY.
YEAH RIGHT, ALIEN BREATH!
EEP!
HEY! WHERE'D SHE GO?
EXCUSE ME.
AGH!
KRAKK!!

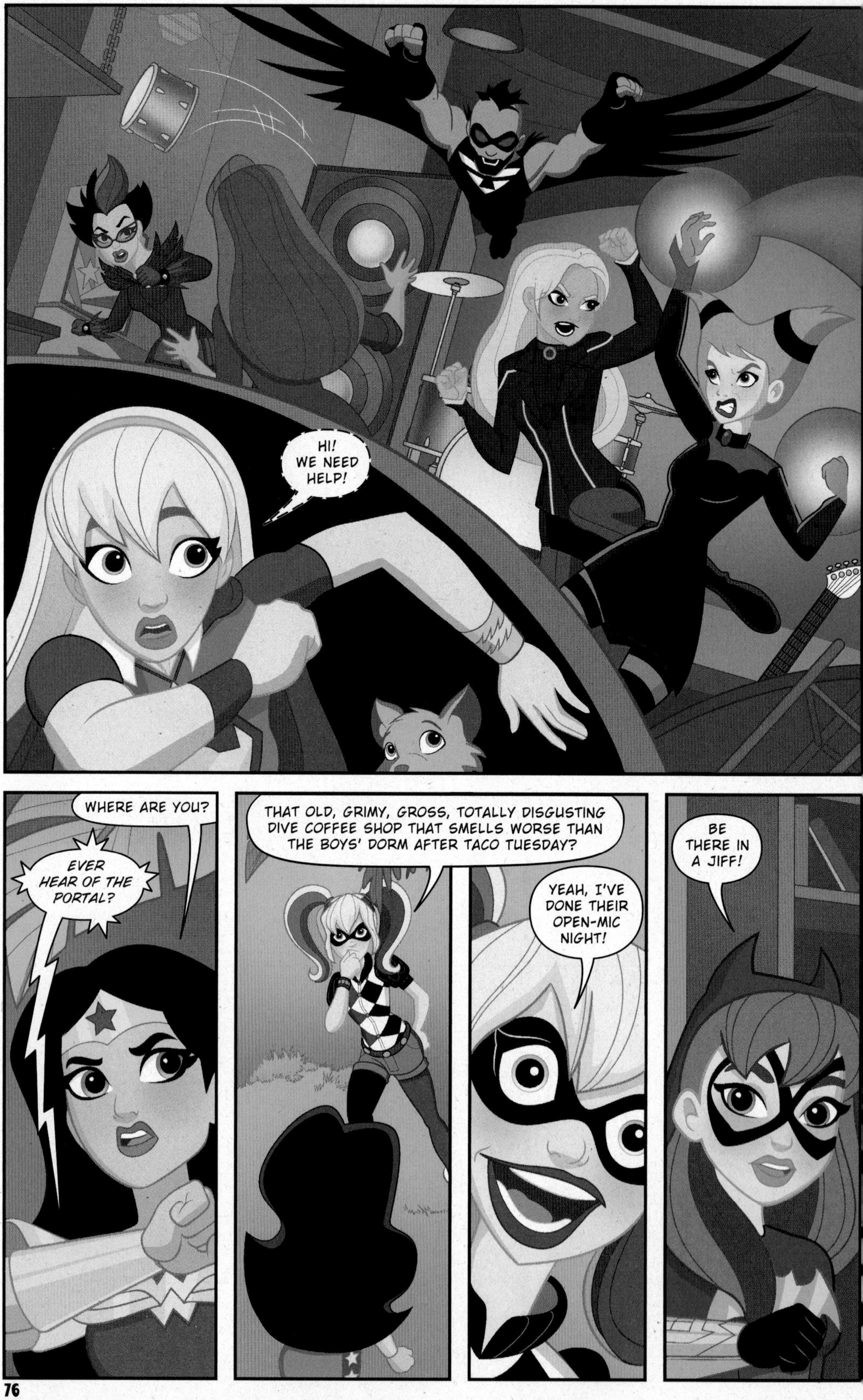
HI! WE NEED HELP!
WHERE ARE YOU?
EVER HEAR OF THE PORTAL?
THAT OLD, GRIMY, GROSS, TOTALLY DISGUSTING DIVE COFFEE SHOP THAT SMELLS WORSE THAN THE BOYS' DORM AFTER TACO TUESDAY?
YEAH, I'VE DONE THEIR OPEN-MIC NIGHT!
BE THERE IN A JIFF!

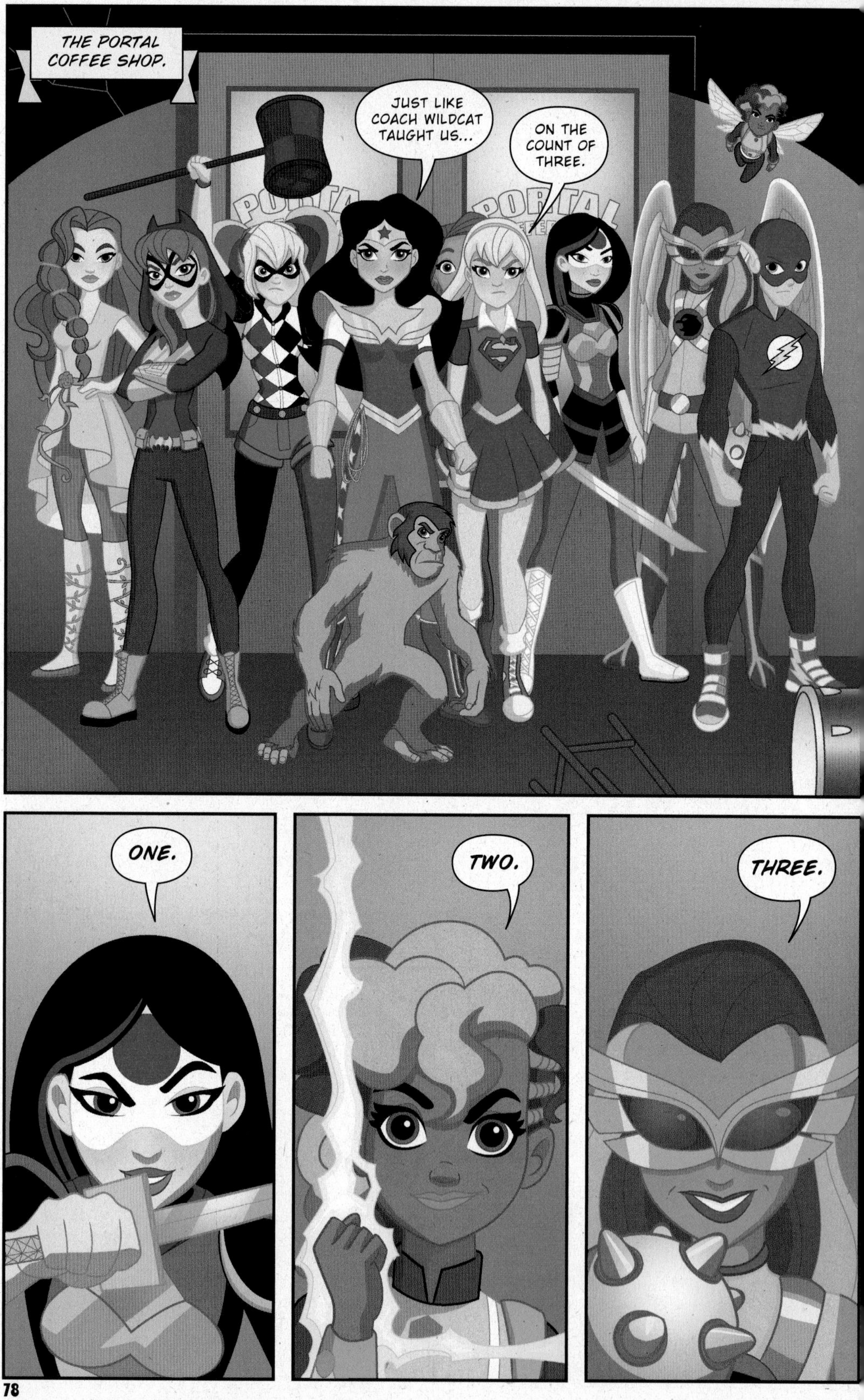
THE PORTAL COFFEE SHOP.
JUST LIKE COACH WILDCAT TAUGHT US...
ON THE COUNT OF THREE.
ONE.
TWO.
THREE.

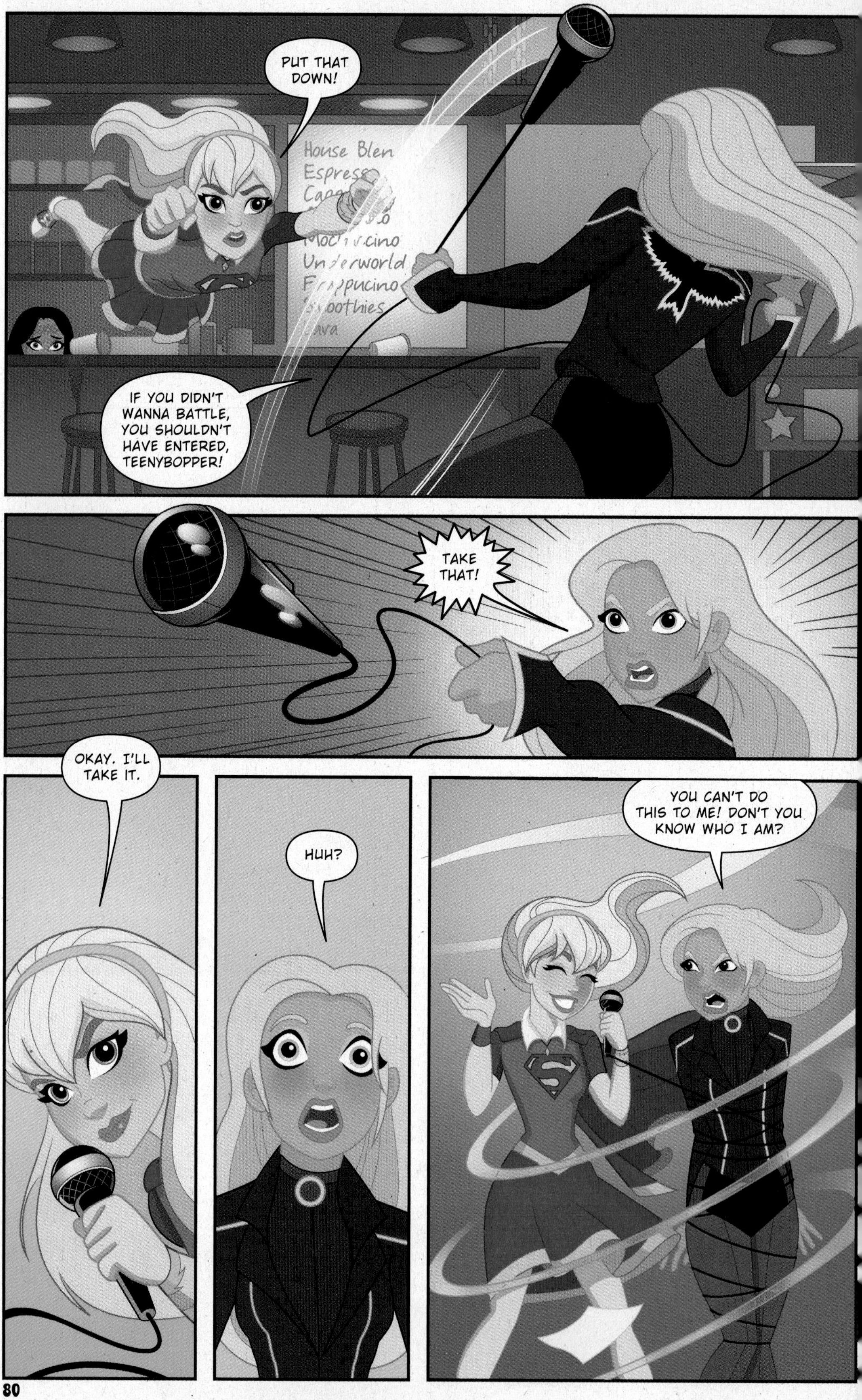
PUT THAT DOWN!
House Blen
Espress
Underworld
Frappucino
IF YOU DIDN'T WANNA BATTLE, YOU SHOULDN'T HAVE ENTERED, TEENYBOPPER!
TAKE THAT!
OKAY. I'LL TAKE IT.
HUH?
YOU CAN'T DO THIS TO ME! DON'T YOU KNOW WHO I AM?

CHAPTER FIVE
THE UNDERWORLD

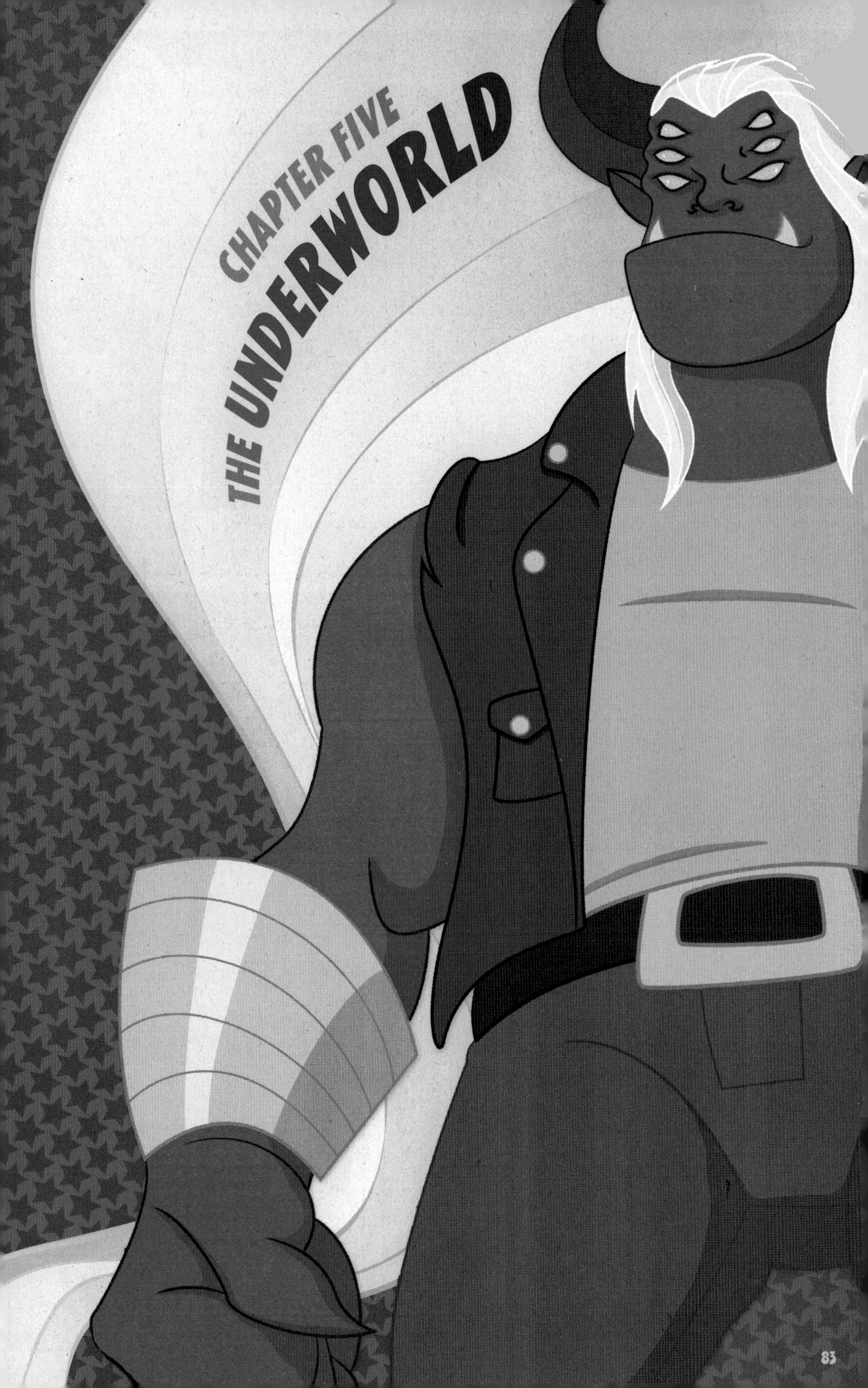

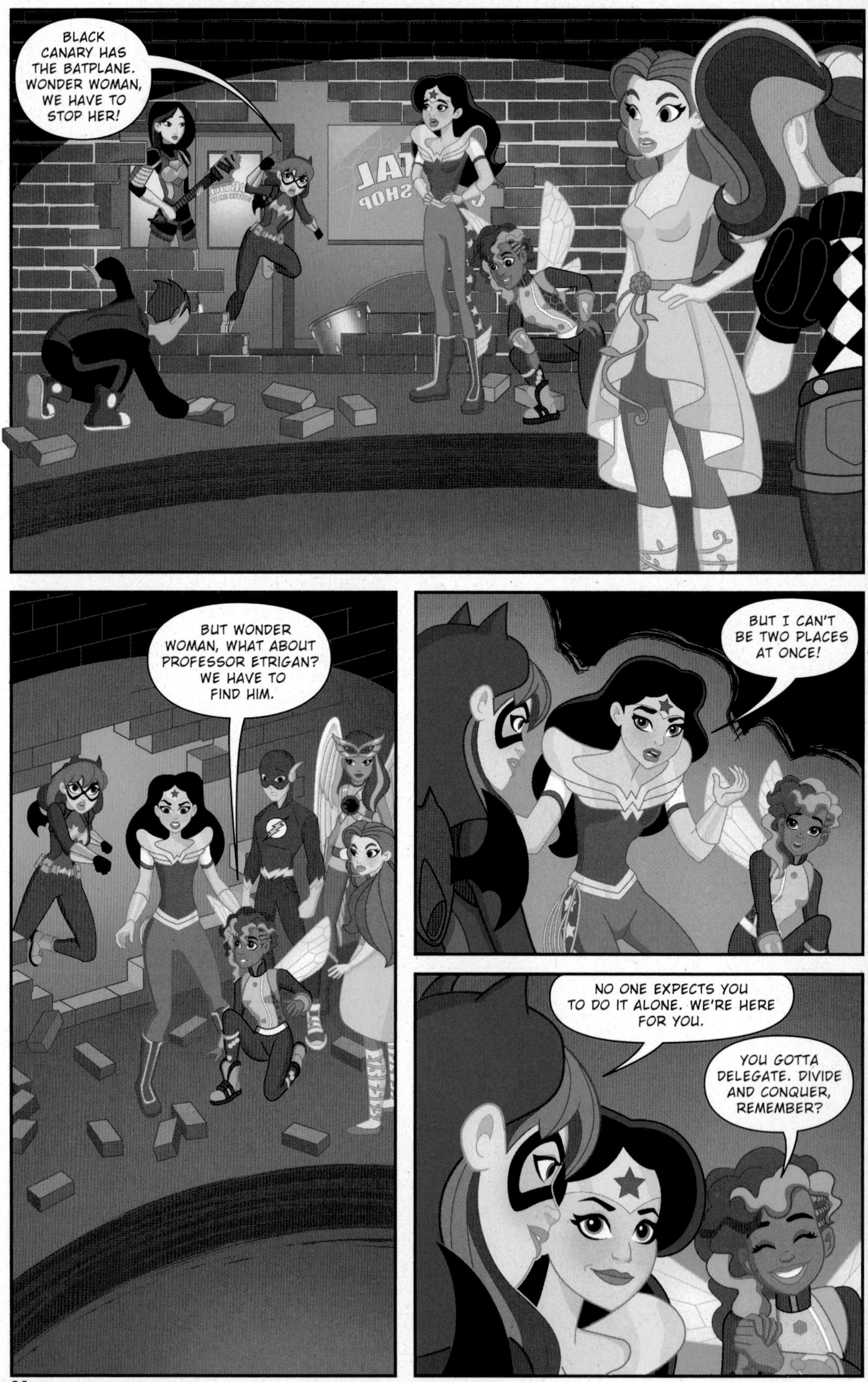
BLACK CANARY HAS THE BATPLANE. WONDER WOMAN, WE HAVE TO STOP HER!
BUT WONDER WOMAN, WHAT ABOUT PROFESSOR ETRIGAN? WE HAVE TO FIND HIM.
BUT I CAN'T BE TWO PLACES AT ONCE!
NO ONE EXPECTS YOU TO DO IT ALONE. WE'RE HERE FOR YOU.
YOU GOTTA DELEGATE. DIVIDE AND CONQUER, REMEMBER?

AAAAAGH!

ÜBER-GNARLY FALL. YOU OKAY?

I MEANT TO DO THAT.

THE UNDERWORLD.

LET'S FIND PROFESSOR ETRIGAN!

EVERYONE STICK TOGETHER--

KLICK!

WHOOSH!

-EEP!- FIRE!

IT'S OKAY, MISS MARTIAN. NO NEED TO TURN INVISIBLE. THE FIRE'S GONE.

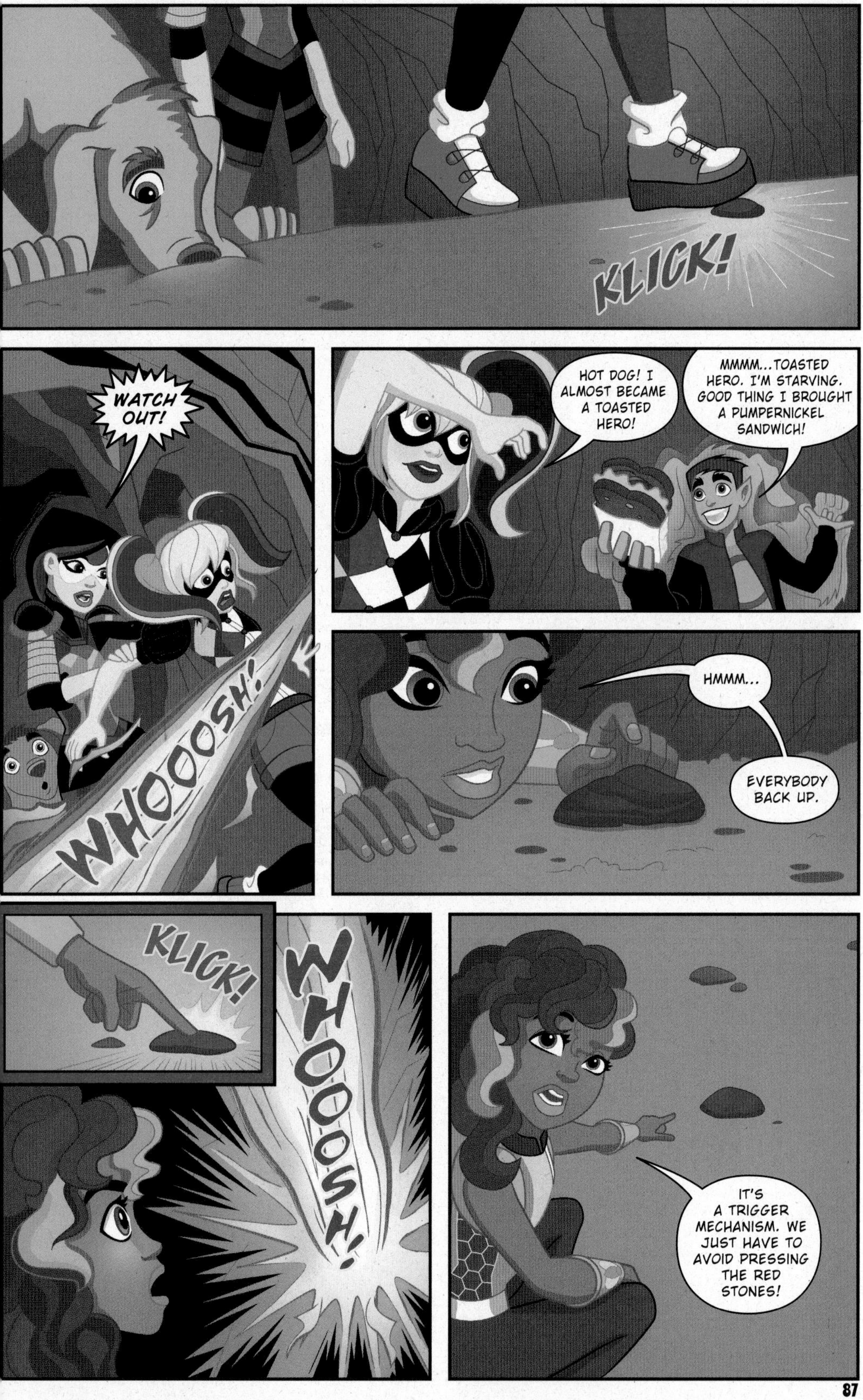
KLICK!
WATCH OUT!
WHOOOOSH!
HOT DOG! I ALMOST BECAME A TOASTED HERO!
MMMM...TOASTED HERO. I'M STARVING. GOOD THING I BROUGHT A PUMPERNICKEL SANDWICH!
HMMM...
EVERYBODY BACK UP.
KLICK!
WHOOOOSH!
IT'S A TRIGGER MECHANISM. WE JUST HAVE TO AVOID PRESSING THE RED STONES!

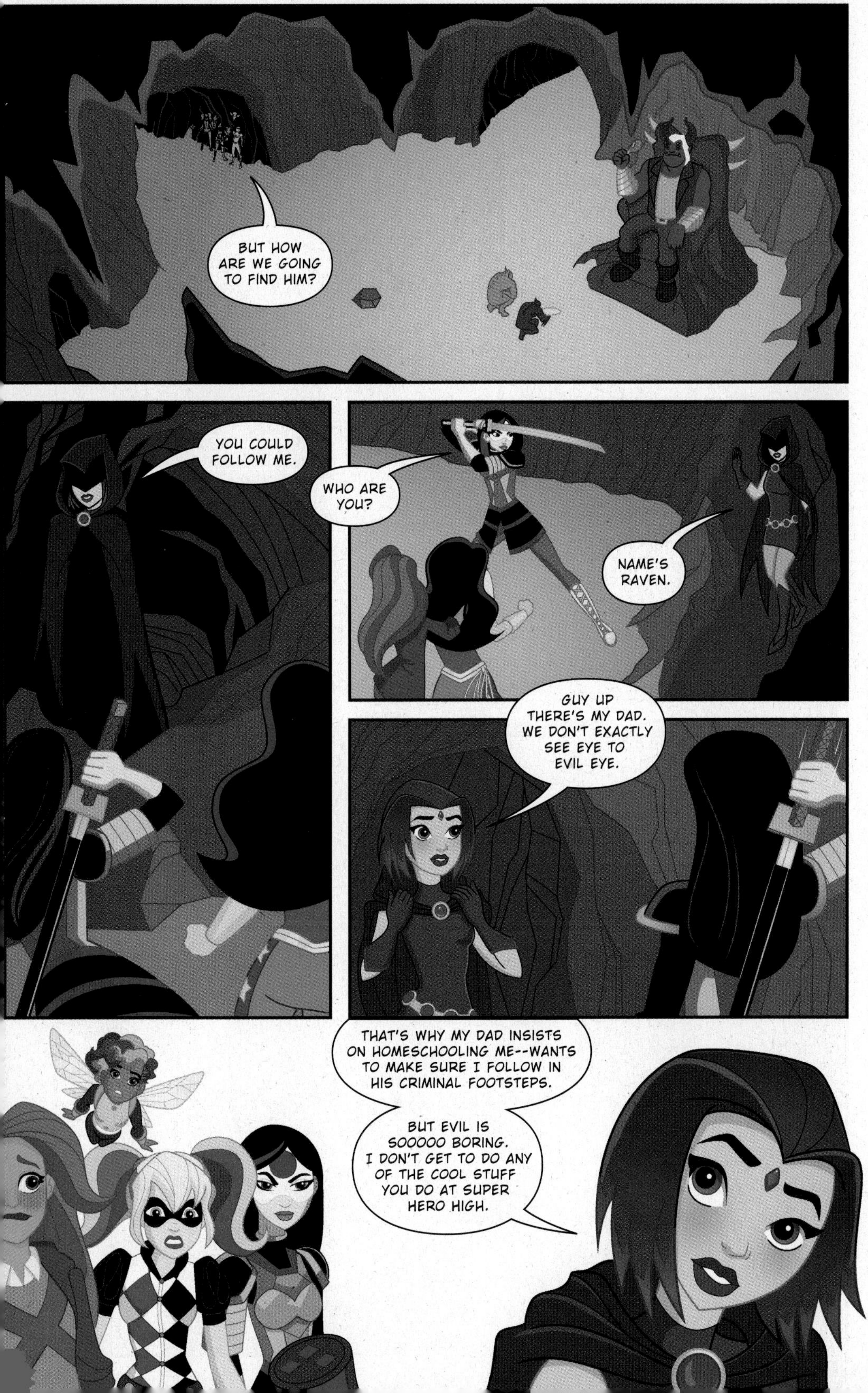
BUT HOW ARE WE GOING TO FIND HIM?
YOU COULD FOLLOW ME.
WHO ARE YOU?
NAME'S RAVEN.
GUY UP THERE'S MY DAD. WE DON'T EXACTLY SEE EYE TO EVIL EYE.
THAT'S WHY MY DAD INSISTS ON HOMESCHOOLING ME--WANTS TO MAKE SURE I FOLLOW IN HIS CRIMINAL FOOTSTEPS.
BUT EVIL IS SOOOOO BORING. I DON'T GET TO DO ANY OF THE COOL STUFF YOU DO AT SUPER HERO HIGH.

91

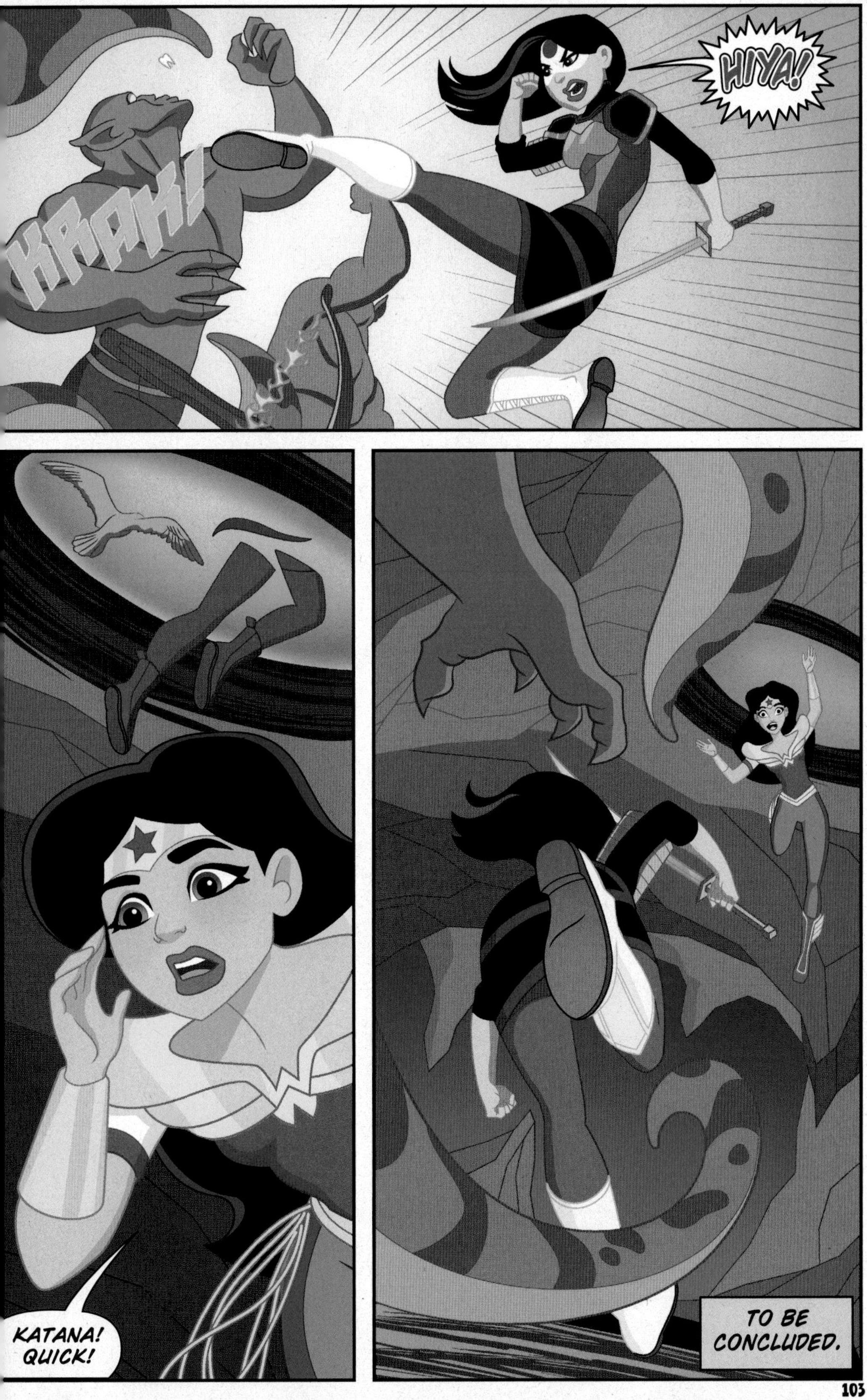
HIYA!
KRAK!
KATANA! QUICK!
TO BE CONCLUDED.

CHAPTER SIX
THE RETURN HOME

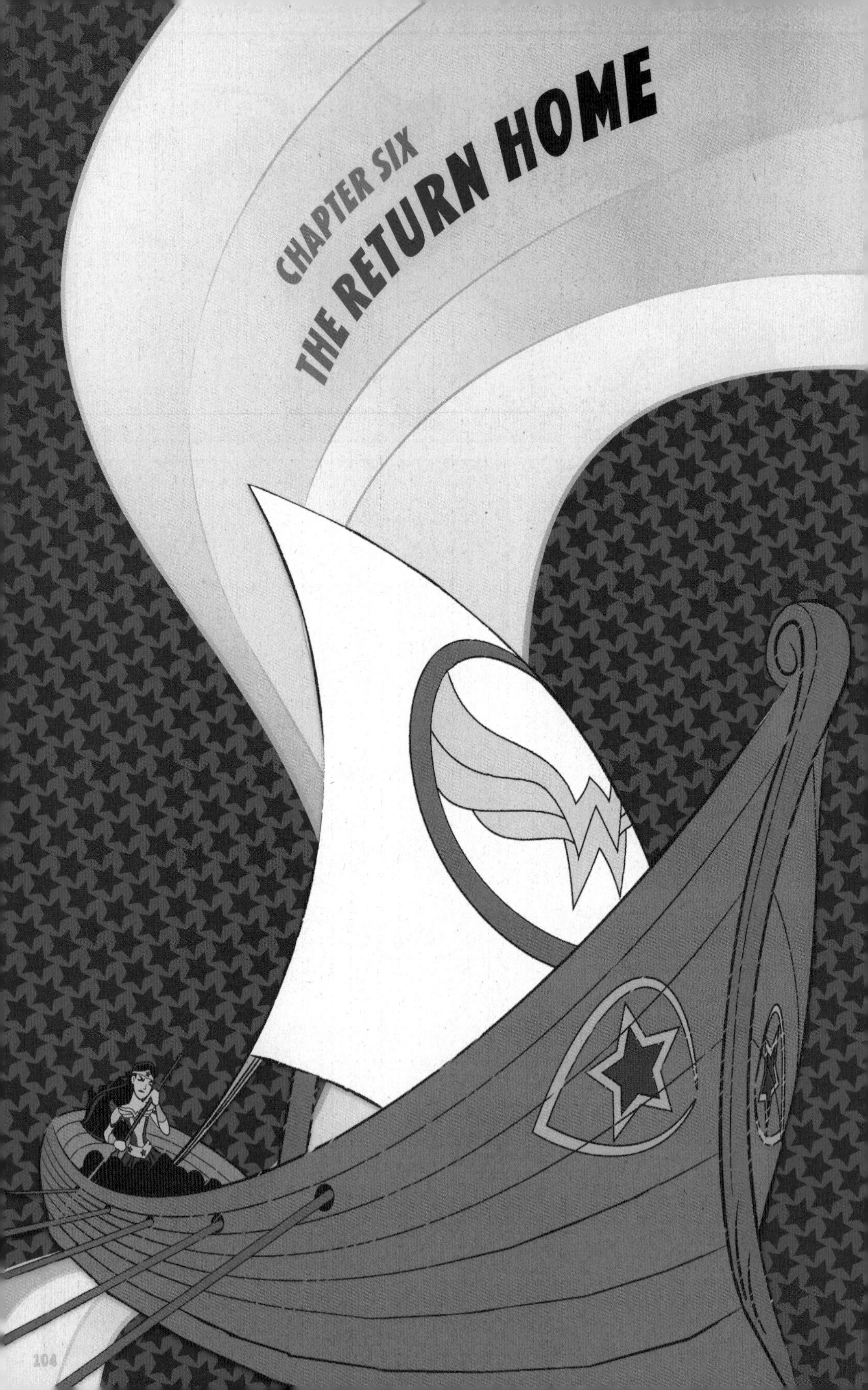

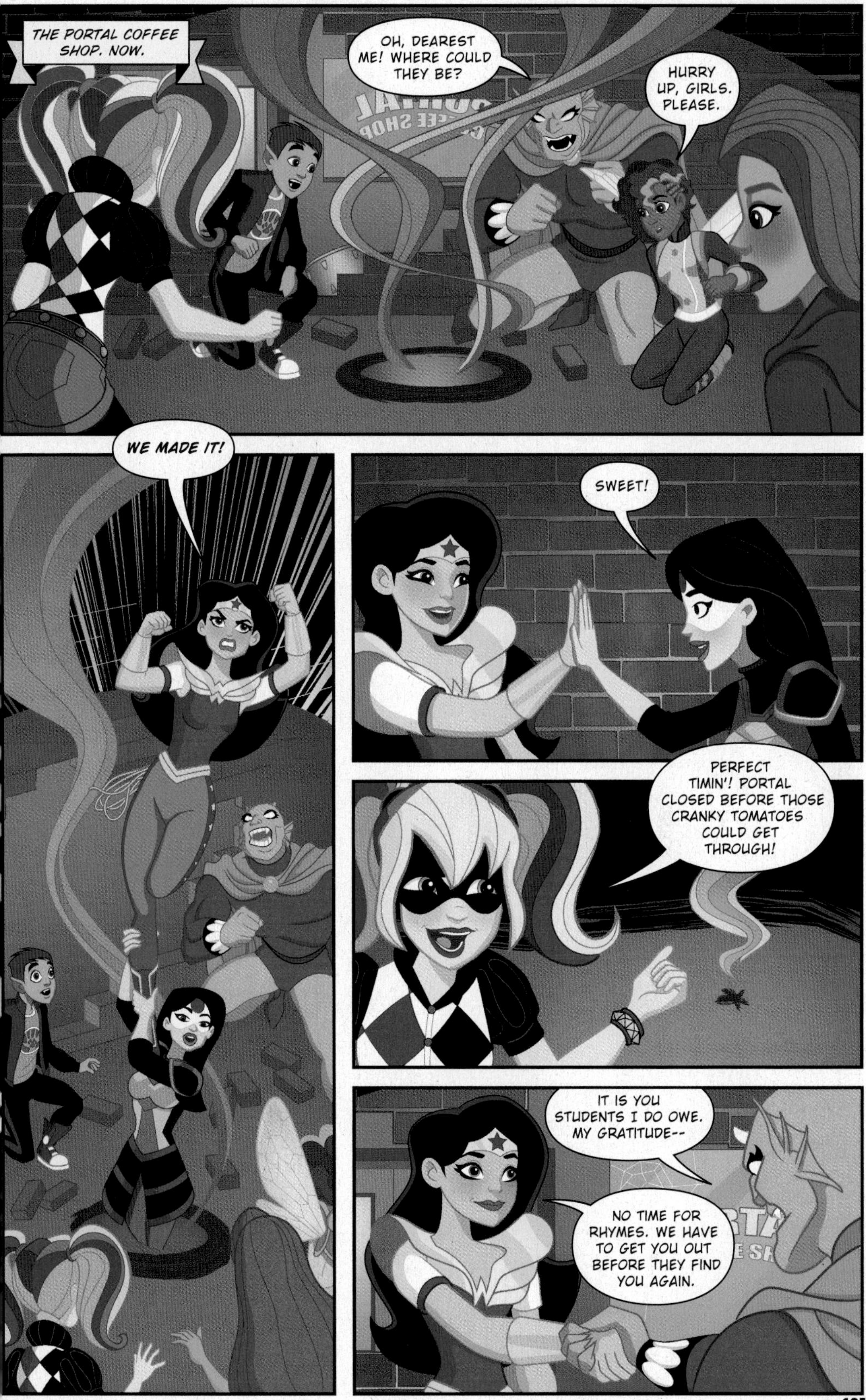

THE PORTAL COFFEE SHOP. NOW.
OH, DEAREST ME! WHERE COULD THEY BE?
HURRY UP, GIRLS. PLEASE.
WE MADE IT!
SWEET!
PERFECT TIMIN'! PORTAL CLOSED BEFORE THOSE CRANKY TOMATOES COULD GET THROUGH!
IT IS YOU STUDENTS I DO OWE. MY GRATITUDE--
NO TIME FOR RHYMES. WE HAVE TO GET YOU OUT BEFORE THEY FIND YOU AGAIN.

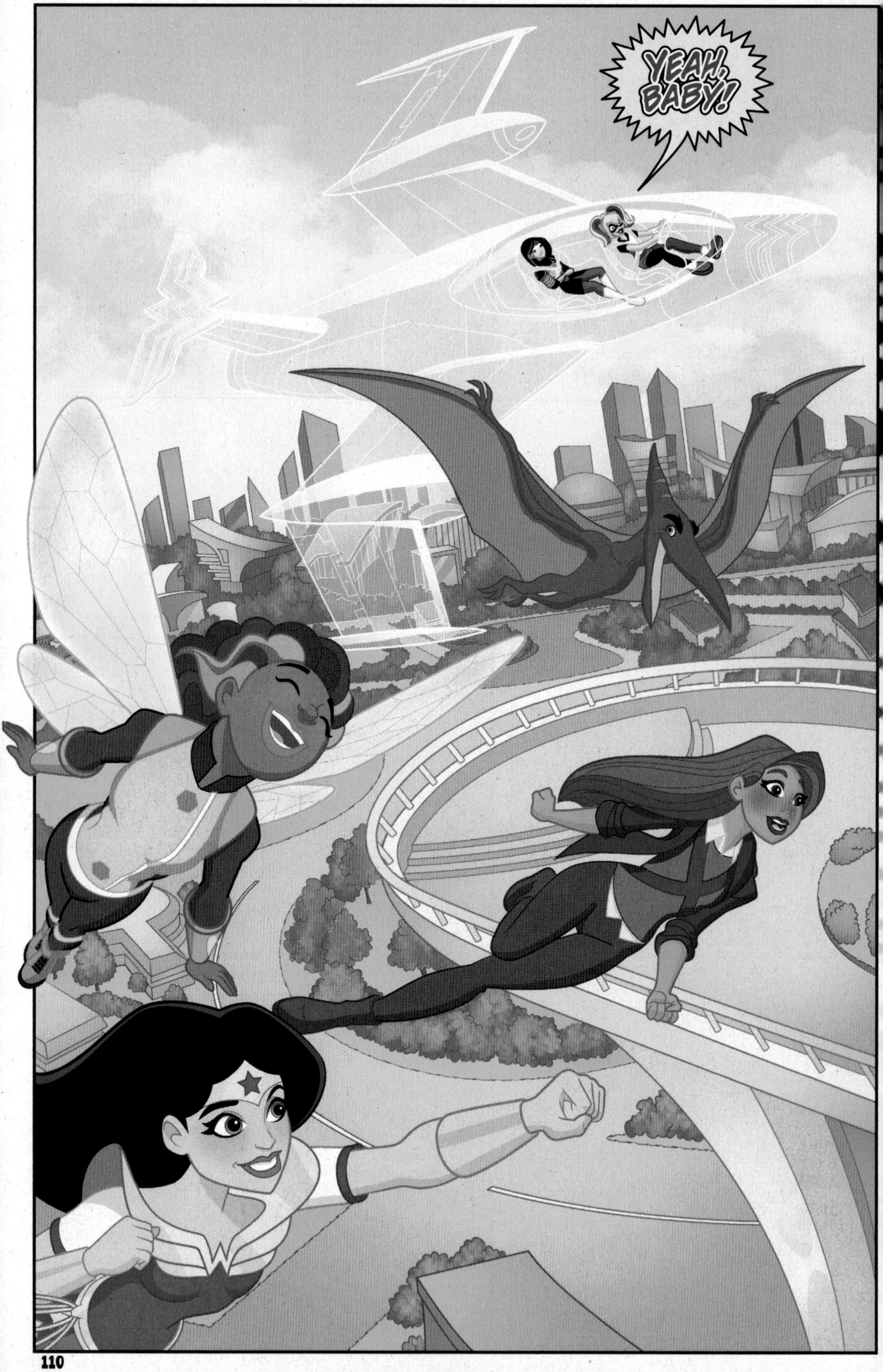
YEAH, BABY!

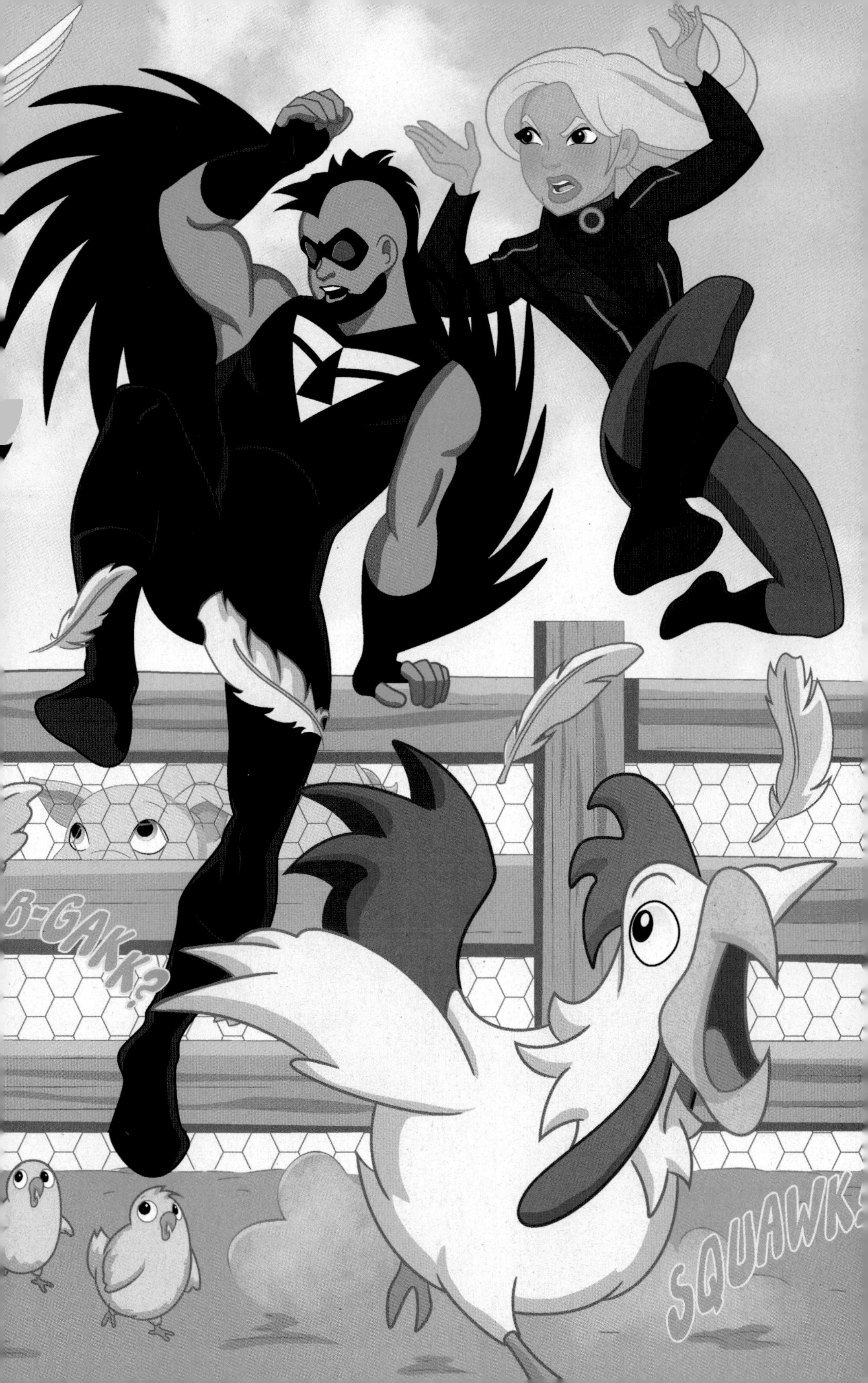
B-GAKK?
SQUAWK

118

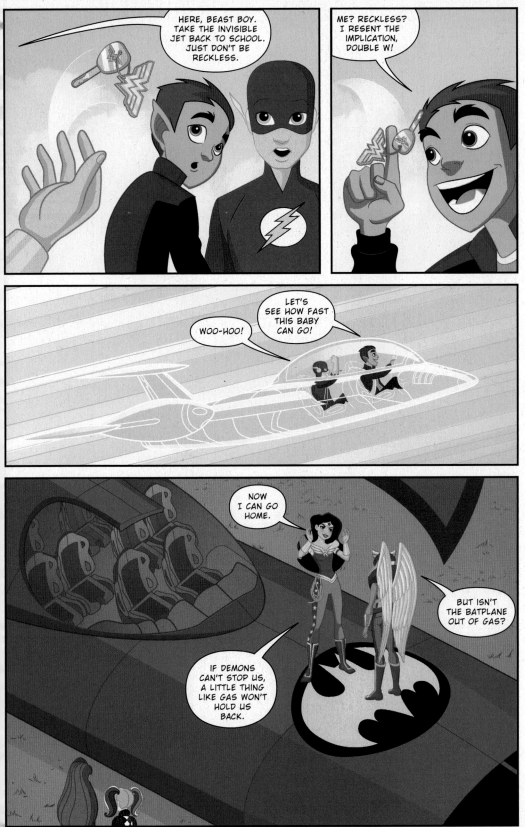

BYE! HAVE FUN AT YOUR SLUMBER PARTY!

BE SURE TO CALL WHEN YOU GET THERE!

THEMYSCIRA.

WELCOME, PRINCESS!

I'M GLAD TO BE HOME, MOM.

WOW, WHAT A PARTY!

NICE DIGS, QUEEN H!

NOW TO COMMENCE THE ALL-NIGHT GAMES, MOVIES AND BRAIDIN' EACH OTHERS' HAIR MARATHON!

THE LITTLE MERA-MAID

LASSO OF TRUTH OR DARE

MISTER TWISTER

PARTY POOPERS.

ZZZZZ...

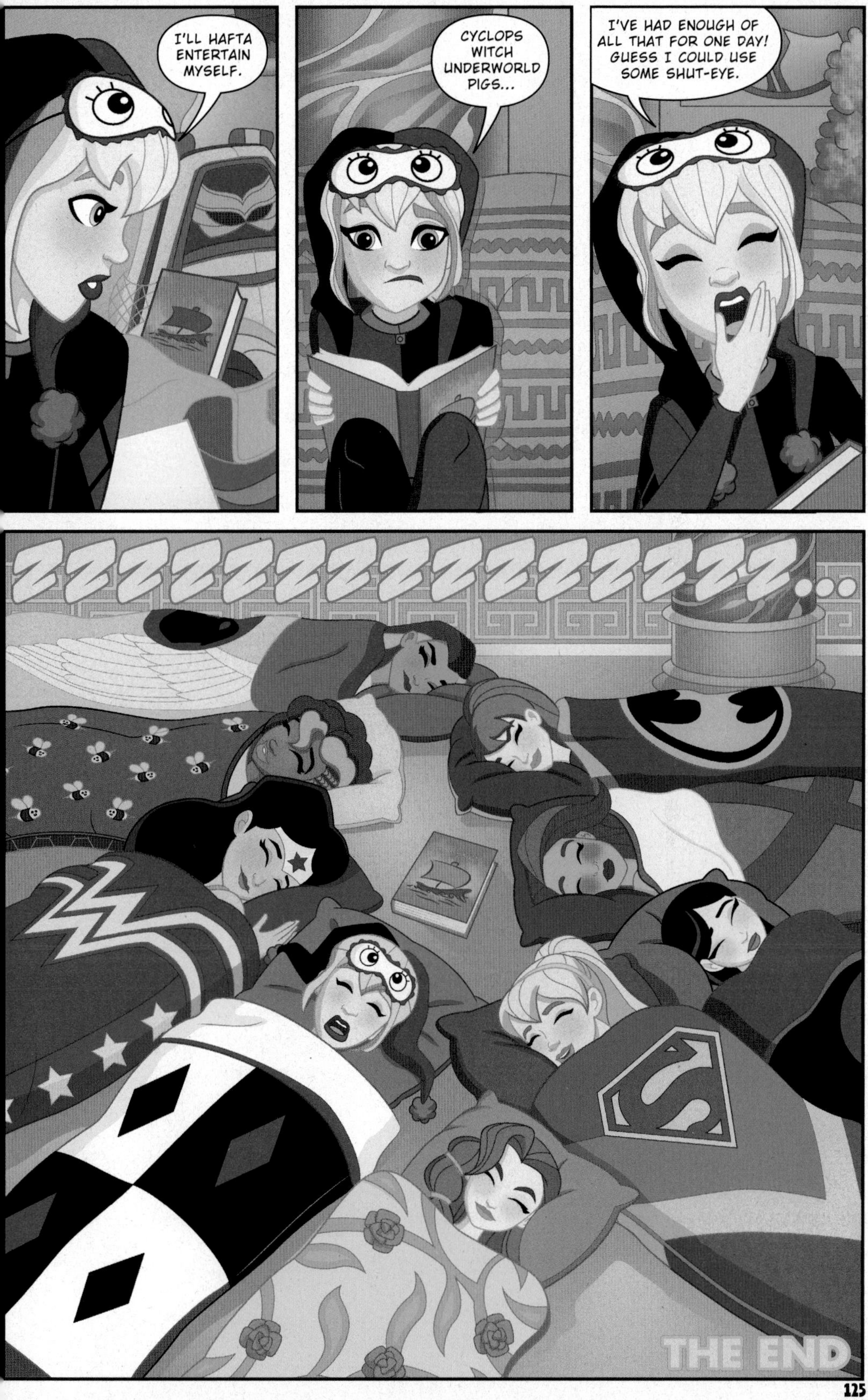
I'LL HAFTA ENTERTAIN MYSELF.
CYCLOPS WITCH UNDERWORLD PIGS...
I'VE HAD ENOUGH OF ALL THAT FOR ONE DAY! GUESS I COULD USE SOME SHUT-EYE.
ZZZZZZZZZZZZZZZ...
THE END

ABOUT THE AUTHOR

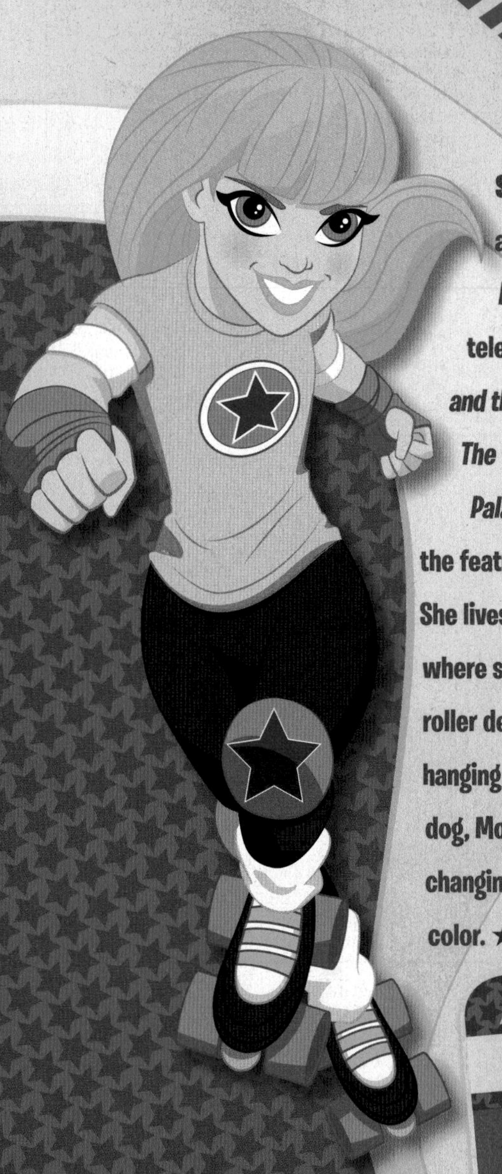

Shea Fontana is a writer for film, television, and graphic novels. Her credits include *DC Super Hero Girls* animated shorts, television specials, and movies, *Dorothy and the Wonders of Oz, Doc McStuffins, The 7D, Whisker Haven Tales with the Palace Pets, Disney on Ice,* and the feature film *Crowning Jules.* She lives in sunny Los Angeles where she enjoys playing roller derby, hiking, hanging out with her dog, Moxie, and changing her hair color. ★

ABOUT THE COLORIST

Monica Kubina

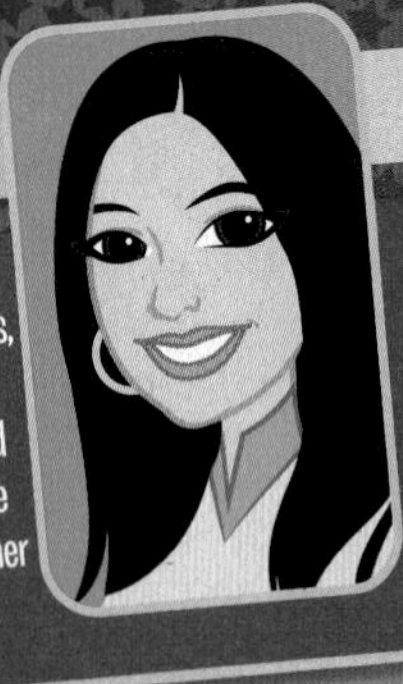

has colored countless comics, including super hero series, manga titles, kids comics, and science fiction stories. She's colored *Phineas and Ferb, SpongeBob, THE 99,* and *Star Wars.* Monica's favorite activities are bike riding and going to museums with her husband and two young sons.

ABOUT THE ARTIST

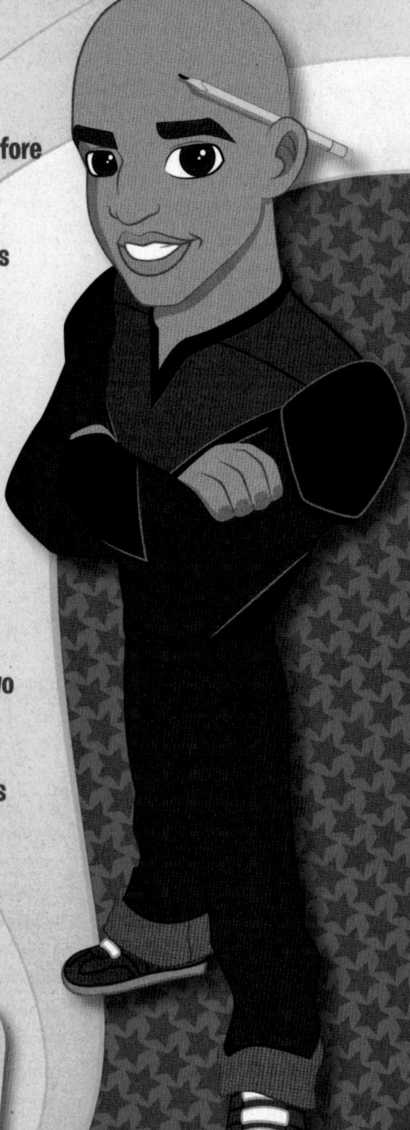

Yancey Labat got his start at Marvel Comics before moving on to illustrate children's books from *Hello Kitty* to *Peanuts* for Scholastic, as well as books for Chronicle Books, ABC Mouse, and others. His book *How Many Jellybeans?* with writer Andrea Menotti won the 2013 Cook Prize for best STEM (Science, Technology, Education, Math) picture book from Bank Street College of Education. He has two super hero girls of his own and lives in Cupertino, California. ★

ABOUT THE LETTERER

Janice Chiang

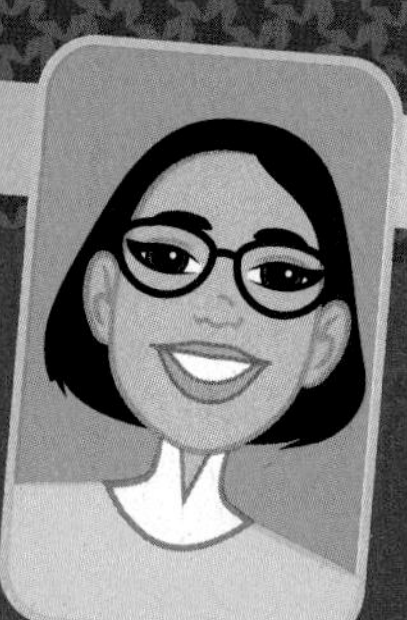

has lettered *Archie, Barbie, Punisher* and many more. She was the first woman to win the Comic Buyer's Guide Fan Awards for Best Letterer (2011). She likes weight training, hiking, baking, gardening, and traveling.

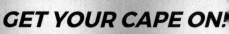

www.**dcsuperherogirls**.com

Follow the adventure:

Get to know the **SUPER HEROES** of Metropolis and watch all-new

GET YOUR CAPE ON!